THE SHEIKH'S FOOLISH PROMISE

PROMISE

GREEN-EYED SHEIKHS BOOK TWO

♥

YASMIN PORTER

Dear Reader,

Thank you so much for picking up my new novel, *The Sheikh's FoolishPromise*! I had a lot of fun writing it, and I hope that you fall in love with the al Abbas family just like I did. **Please join my mailing list** (http://eepurl.com/be56-1) so that I can let you know as soon as the next volume in *The Green-Eyed Sheikhs* series is available. Subscribers get inside info about special promotions, plus they get the chance to enter my monthly giveaways.

1

Katherine Delaney squinted her eyes against the glaring afternoon sun and adjusted her sunglasses. Her old pickup truck rumbled along the dirt road, bouncing off of rocks and divots, jumbling her in her seat. Banjo, the old mutt she'd found begging for scraps down at the market, groaned and rolled onto his side, raising one paw to block the light from his eyes.

It must have been at least a hundred degrees outside. She could see waves of heat shimmering off the road in the distance, and the sun was so bright that she definitely wouldn't have been able to see clearly if she took off her shades. The truck's air conditioning was shot, and she had both windows rolled all the way down in an effort to get some fresh air circulating.

Only the thin layer of sweat that covered her body kept her cool. She took a long gulp of water from the Nalgene bottle that she always kept with her and offered some to the dog. He picked up his head, lapped at the thin stream she poured onto his lips, then went right back to sleep.

She must have been hallucinating. It wouldn't have been the first time that her eyes had played tricks on her in the desert. She tried to stay hydrated so that she didn't get disoriented, especially while driving, but the heat made her so sleepy and the way the intense desert light reflected off the sand sometimes made her see things that weren't there.

This was the first time it had made her see a motorcycle. At least, she thought she was looking at a motorcycle. It was still too far off in the distance for her to be certain, and the longer she drove, the further it seemed to be.

She couldn't recall having seen a bike since she had arrived in Samarra a month prior. Most of the roads she'd traveled, especially those that led out to her site, were unpaved. People drove vehicles with four wheel drive, or else they walked or rode pack animals. A motorcycle would have been pretty impractical, since it offered no protection from the sun.

The closer she got, the more certain she became that she really was seeing a bike by the side of the road. She drove toward it, not that she had any choice. The road she was on stretched directly from her site to the nearest village with a market, approximately thirty kilometers away. It was a straight shot with no cross traffic, and usually she was the only person on the road.

There wasn't much reason for anyone else to be on the road. Katherine was on it almost every other day, since she was constantly inventing reasons that she needed to go into town. She very rarely passed any other travelers, and most of those other travelers were villagers who she now recognized. Sometimes, if they were on foot, she'd give them a lift.

It just got so boring out at her site. Not that she wasn't thrilled to be there; on the contrary, running her own archaeological dig had been a dream of hers since she was a little girl. She loved her work, slowly chiseling her giant winged bulls out of the side of a mountain and exploring the caves behind them. She'd even named them, Fred and Barney, and she sincerely looked forward to seeing them each morning when she woke up.

Still, her tent in Samarra was such a culture shock from her apartment back in New York. Kate loved adventures, but once she settled in to her dig, she found herself craving things from back home. Like potato chips and Netflix.

That's how she found herself at the nearest market several times per week. Despite the fact that it was located in the middle of the desert, the market offered several familiar comforts. Kate was able to stock up on necessities like Nutella and bootleg movies that she could watch on her laptop. She might not have had access to everything she craved, but she did have a pretty good selection of junk food.

Kate pulled up alongside the bike and turned the ignition off. Banjo picked up his head and gave her an inquiring whimper.

"Just a second, bud," she replied, slipping into her long sleeve button up shirt. She usually drove around in a tank top, but the sun was so harsh and her skin was so fair that she needed to cover up every time she stepped out of the shade, even if it was just for a minute. It was one of the many curses of being a natural redhead. She burned up like a lobster if she wasn't careful. Plus ladies weren't supposed to be out in public uncovered in Samarra.

She tucked her curls up into her sun hat and looked around to see whether she could spot the bike's owner. She'd heard stories about women being abducted after they tried to help stranded motorists, and she didn't want to prove her family right. They hadn't been very supportive of her plan to travel to the Middle East. Kate's folks had never been outside of Minnesota, let alone out of the United States. They basically believed that the entire world was populated by evil men whose greatest goal in life was to snatch young ladies.

She didn't see any potential kidnappers. Kate opened the door to the truck and swung her legs out, hopping down to the dusty road. The moment she stepped out into the sun, the heat hit her like a ton of bricks. It was early in the afternoon and she wondered how the bike got to the side of the road. It definitely hadn't been there when she was on her way to the market, which meant that it must have shown up sometime in the past three hours.

She touched it. The black metal was so hot that she burned her finger. She shook her hand and put her finger in her mouth to soothe it. The bike must have been sitting out in the sun for quite a while. It looked old, like maybe it was from the mid-twentieth century, but it was in excellent condition. The paint was a bit dull, but Kate didn't see any rust or damage.

She didn't really know anything at all about motorcycles, but this one looked pretty cool. It had some Russian writing on it and she thought she could see a hitch on one side. Maybe for a sidecar?

Katherine imagined herself tearing down the dirt road with Banjo in a sidecar. She'd never been on a motorcycle before, but it seemed like something she'd enjoy. She loved roller coasters and once she'd ridden a horse and she had really liked that. A motorcycle kind of seemed like a combination of a roller coaster and a horse.

She briefly considered loading the motorcycle into the bed of her truck. She had to dismiss that thought right away, first because she didn't actually want to steal someone's bike, and second, because she never could have lifted it on her own anyways.

Kate felt like she ought to do something with the bike, but she didn't know what. She knew that if she left it, the next person who stumbled upon it would probably take it. She didn't know how much the bike was worth, but she guessed that it was at least enough to feed an average Samarri family for a long time.

If her phone had worked out in the desert, she could have called the base and asked whoever answered for some advice or help. The phone didn't work on the road between camp and the market though. Kate decided that she'd just have to leave the bike and ask for help when she got back to the dig.

She hopped back into the truck and scratched Banjo behind his ears. Kate turned the key in the ignition and continued on her journey, slightly disappointed that she had to leave the bike behind.

It wasn't long before she was rubbing her eyes again. There, on the side of the road up ahead, she saw something else weird. She couldn't quite make out what it was. It was a black form, smaller than the bike, and it appeared to be moving. Was it some kind of animal? A leopard? That didn't make any sense. There were no leopards in Samarra. A dog, maybe? Kate drove toward the shape.

"Holy shit," she muttered under her breath once she was close enough to see what it was. That black shape was a man, crawling on his hands and knees. Kate accelerated to the man and stopped short beside him, accidentally enveloping him in a cloud of dust.

"Sorry! Sorry," she yelled as she jumped out of her truck. The man coughed and covered his eyes. He was wearing jeans, boots, and a leather biker's jacket.

He muttered something in Arabic and collapsed onto his side. Kate swept his shoulder-length hair out of his eyes. He was covered in sweat, but it was already dried and he was burning up. This was a bad sign. It meant that the biker was severely dehydrated.

"Wait here!" She ran back to the truck and got her water bottle. She brought it to the man's parted lips. "Drink slowly," she instructed, pouring a few drops into his mouth.

The biker lapped at the water, and once he

recognized what it was, he grabbed the bottle from Kate's hands.

"Don't gulp!" she tried to warn him, afraid he'd choke or make himself sick. He wasn't listening though. He poured the water down his throat until he was coughing some back up. "Slowly," she admonished him, holding his hands while he made smaller sips.

"You need to get out of this jacket," she told him. "You're burning up. Come on." Kate helped the guy out of the leather coat. The white T-shirt he wore underneath was soaked through with sweat. She poured a little of the water over the back of his neck.

"You speak English?" the man finally asked. His eyes weren't focused and Kate knew that he was probably feeling pretty awful. She wondered how long he'd been out in the sun and what the hell he was doing out in the middle of nowhere in the desert.

Was this guy Samarri? He had the tawny skin and aquiline nose that she'd come to associate with the Samarri people, but his eyes were bright green. Plus he was dressed like a biker from the 1950s. Katherine looked her new friend over as he sipped water and recovered his strength. He smelled a little ripe, but even in his current condition, there was no denying that he was gorgeous.

He was huge, probably nearly six and a half feet tall when he stood, and she could make out every single one of his muscles beneath his wet T-shirt. She guessed that he was a little older than her, probably in his early thirties.

"Yes," she answered, wetting the sleeve of her shirt and wiping the dry sweat from his brow. "Can you stand?"

"Where is your father?" the man replied, looking around and trying to focus his vision.

"Excuse me?" Kate guessed that the guy might have been delirious. She wasn't a doctor, at least not that kind of doctor, and she couldn't really tell how much danger he was in.

"Your father. Is he in the truck?"

"No, just my dog."

"Did you steal this truck from him? Do you

know how to drive it?"

"What? No, I didn't steal the truck." *I wanted to steal your motorcycle, but I didn't steal that either*, Kate thought to herself.

"You're trying to tell me that a boy your age has his own truck?"

Katherine rolled her eyes, sighed, and lifted up her sun hat so that her red curls fell to her shoulders.

"A woman!" the man exclaimed. "Wow. You don't look like a woman. You're so small. Where is your husband?"

"Oh for God's sake," Kate groaned. "Just get in the truck."

2

It wasn't the first time in Katherine's adult life that someone had mistaken her for a prepubescent boy. She was just barely five feet tall, and like her mother and her sisters, she hadn't exactly been blessed by the boob fairy. When she was younger, she tried to compensate for her slight, boyish figure by putting on makeup and always wearing dresses.

Unfortunately, her mother didn't have any makeup skills to pass down to her daughters either. With her red hair and freckles, more often than not, Kate ended up looking like a clown when she wore makeup rather than a sophisticated lady. By the time she'd hit graduate school, she'd given up on things like eyeliner and heavily pigmented lipsticks in favor of simple mascara and lip gloss. Since she'd been in Samarra, she hadn't even bothered with that.

Kate would describe her work clothes in Samarra as "archaeological dig casual." She usually wore jeans or khaki cargo pants with white tank tops and hiking boots. When she went into town, she'd throw on a white, button-up men's shirt. And of course she wouldn't be caught dead in the desert sun without her sunglasses and sun hat.

Still, she didn't particularly like being mistaken for a kid, and she didn't like that question about her husband either. She decided not to hold it against the guy. It probably was very strange for him to encounter a foreign woman driving alone through the desert, plus he was obviously not in his right mind.

Ever since she'd managed to wrangle him into the truck, he'd not said a word. He was panting a little bit and every so often he took little sips out of Kate's water bottle. She glanced at him from the corner of her eye and he looked a little greenish.

"Are you doing okay?" she asked. "Are you gonna be sick? I can pull over for a second if you need to rest."

The guy just shook his head no. He had his head propped up in one hand and his other hand was buried in Banjo's fur, scratching the dog gently between the ears.

"Okay, we're almost there," Katherine continued, feeling bad for the guy. She wanted to chat with him, to ask him what he was doing out there alone, but he didn't seem like he was up for any conversation. She drove back to the camp a little faster than usual, in part because she was worried about him and in part because she was excited about her find.

It didn't take them too long to arrive. Kate pulled into her usual parking place. "Stay here, I'm gonna get some help."

She jogged into the break tent with Banjo at her heels. "I need help!" she announced before looking to see who was there. "I've found a man!"

"Congratulations?" Kate heard Jarrod Cole, the other lead researcher on her team answer, his voice dripping with sarcasm. Ugh. That guy was such a twat. She ignored him and addressed Mike Cavannaugh, one of the grad student assistants.

"I found a guy broken down on the side of the road. He's dehydrated, but I think he's gonna be okay. Can you help me to get him into a bed? I think he needs to cool down and rest."

Mike followed her out to the truck. "What was he doing out there?" he asked, extending his stride to keep up with her.

"I don't know," Kate answered. "I think he might be Samarri, but I'm not one hundred percent sure."

"That's weird he'd be out on our road if he wasn't headed to us. Was he in a truck?"

"Motorcycle," Kate answered, showing Mike to her own truck. "Here he is."

She opened the door slowly and Mike helped the guy to his feet. "You okay, bro?" The younger man wrapped the biker's arm around his shoulders. "Should I take him to your tent?"

"I guess so," Kate answered. They didn't have a designated first aid tent, so hers was as good as any. Plus, she didn't know why she was feeling this way, but she trusted the guy. He looked like a huge, burly biker dude but something about his deep voice and bright green eyes made her feel safe. She wanted to take care of him.

Once they arrived at her tent, Mike helped the guy to lay on his back on top of Kate's thin blanket. "What should we do?" he asked Kate. "Do you think someone should try to get a hold of a doctor?"

"I'm okay," the guy answered. "I just need

to rest for a minute. I'm already feeling much better."

"Are you sure, dude?" Mike tilted his head to one side.

The guy grinned. "I'm sure, dude," he answered. "I'm just going to chill out here a minute and I'll be on my way. Oh! Is my bike okay?"

Mike looked to Kate for clarification.

"It's by the side of the road about fifteen kilometers down."

"Shit. I'm an idiot. I ran out of petrol. I'm sorry to have to ask you this, but do you think you could send someone to get it? I inherited that bike from my father and I'd hate to lose it. I promise that I'll be forever in your debt."

"I can pick it up if I can borrow the truck," Mike answered. Kate tossed him the keys and he was on his way.

"So," Kate addressed her patient. "I'm Kate." She held out her hand. Her patient smiled and gave her a firm shake.

"Kaliq. Thank you for rescuing me. I

apologize if I said anything offensive. I guess I can behave like a real ass when I'm low on fluids."

"Oh, you weren't... that bad," Kate pursed her lips.

"Honestly, I think I may have been hallucinating. I just really wasn't expecting to encounter a woman on the road. Are you American?"

"Yep, Minnesota born and raised. And you? You can't be Samarri, right?"

"Actually I am," Kaliq smiled. "Half at least. But I went to school in New York."

"It just so happens that I also went to school in New York," Kate raised her eyebrows. "Columbia?"

"NYU. What are you doing out here?"

"This is my dig," Kate couldn't help but to smile when she said that. She knew it was a bit childish, but she was so proud of her site.

"Really? The lamassu, you mean? Your dig as in..."

"I'm in charge here," Kate nodded still smiling. For some reason, she was pleased that

Kaliq already knew the proper name of the two winged bulls she was unearthing.

"Wow. You look really young."

"It's a blessing and a curse, I guess," Kate replied.

"Don't try to tell me you're a day over thirty. I wouldn't believe it."

"Well, you would be right to doubt me. I'm twenty nine. This is actually the first time I've led a dig on my own," Kate admitted.

"Incredible!"

Kate knew that she was blushing. Usually guys like Kaliq weren't interested in girls like her. He was so handsome and charming, now that he was no longer dying. She was pretty sure that he was flirting with her, but her lack of experience with hot men kept her from responding. She knew that she sort of had a tendency to stick her foot in her mouth and she didn't want to say something dumb and embarrass herself. "By the way," she remembered, "what were you doing out there? That road doesn't go anywhere for hundreds of kilometers."

"That's not true," he gave her that thousand watt smile again. "That road leads to this dig. I was actually on my way here. I'd heard about the lamassu and I wanted to see for myself."

"Oh!" Kate's face brightened. "Are you an ancient history enthusiast?"

"Actually," Kaliq corrected her, "I'm an artist myself."

"Ah," Kate nodded. "I could see that."

"You could see that I'm an artist?"

"You kind of have a rock star look going on."

"Is that a good thing?"

"I didn't leave you by the side of the road, did I?" Kate laughed.

"So can I see them?" Kaliq's voice dropped.

Kate's eyes nearly bugged out of her head. "See what?" God, he looked so hot there, lying in her bed.

Kaliq leaned closer toward her and she found herself involuntarily leaning toward him in response. "The lamassu," he said in a softer voice.

"Oh. The lamassu. Of course." She knew that her disappointment was probably audible. *Jeez*, she thought. *What was this guy doing to her?* Since when was she not interested in showing off the winged bulls she'd dug up?

Kaliq sat up in bed and winced.

"Whoa!" Katherine noticed. "Maybe you aren't completely recovered yet. You don't look so good." That was a lie, he looked incredible. He also looked like he might pass out or vomit though. "Here," she added, handing him a full bottle of water. "Drink this."

"Sorry. I felt fine, then when I sat up, my head was spinning again." Kaliq sipped on his water.

"Well, how about this. You stay here and get some rest. We can feed you and you can spend the night recuperating, then you can see Fred and Barney in the morning."

"Okay," Kaliq agreed. "Who are Fred and Barney?"

"The lamassu," Kate answered with a

slight cringe. "We named them Fred and Barney." Actually, she had named them that herself, but she didn't want Kaliq to know what a dork she was.

"Prehistoric names. Totally appropriate. I don't think you need to worry about me though. I'm sure that I'll be okay in just a minute."

"Is your wife waiting for you to get home?" Kate hoped that was as subtle as she intended.

Kaliq grinned. "I'm not married. I do have several nervous aunties though. They might miss me if they were expecting me, but I live alone. Wait," he looked at Kate from the corner of his eye, "you're not planning to kidnap me, are you?"

"I don't know," Kate replied. "Are you worth big bucks? It's very expensive to run an archaeological dig. Do you think your aunties would be willing to spring for your release?"

"Hmm," Kaliq pretended to consider Kate's question. "If you'd have grabbed my older brother, I'd say definitely. I can't promise you that you'd be able to extort money from them in exchange for me. They might try to offer you some tea or halva or something in exchange for my safe return."

"No deal," Kate shook her head.

"Well." Kaliq put his hands behind his head. "I guess that means I'm at your mercy."

Katherine wished that he really was at her mercy. If everything were up to her, she would have none. She'd keep him up all night long if she could, kissing that adorable smirk right off of his face. Her eyes traveled down his face toward his chest, where his T-shirt still clung to him. "Hey," she realized. "You want a clean shirt? I'm sure we have a clean T-shirt that will fit you around here somewhere."

"That would be nice."

Katherine loped off to borrow a shirt from Mike, who was about the same size as Kaliq. She returned with some dinner for the two of them, plus a few extra blankets.

"Here," she tossed Kaliq the T-shirt, then stood and stared at him like an idiot. "I'm sorry," she realized, "you probably want some privacy to change."

"Are you worried about offending my modesty?" Kaliq laughed, peeling off the dirty shirt. "I haven't got any." He paused for a moment while Kate gawked at him before pulling the clean shirt over his head.

"Can I offer you some sandwiches?" Kate held a paper plate out to Kaliq in an attempt to change the subject. She sat down on the bed beside him and helped herself to a peanut butter and jelly. Judging by the way things were going, it was going to be a long night, and that was perfectly fine with her.

3

"So," Kate started, "I guess we should probably turn in."

Kaliq was still in her bed. Or *on* it, rather, since he hadn't actually made his way underneath of the covers. His massive body took up nearly the entire cot, which was a simple metal frame with a thin mattress. His feet dangled off the end even though his head was on her pillow.

"Okay," he replied. "I guess it's getting late." He didn't move.

Kate didn't know quite how to proceed. The camp didn't get many overnight guests, and they didn't have any free cots. She was getting pretty sleepy, but Kaliq wasn't going anywhere. There wasn't anywhere for him to go even if he had wanted to move.

She stretched and yawned, hoping he'd get the hint.

"Am I in your bed right now?"

"Um, actually you kind of are."

"Ah!" Kaliq began to get up but winced slightly again. "I'll just sleep on the floor."

"That's not necessary!" Kate rushed to respond, putting her hand on his chest and pushing him back down. He was still so warm. She hadn't intended to touch him, but once she had her hand on him, she couldn't bear to remove it. He felt so solid, and something about his mass gave Kate butterflies in her stomach.

Kaliq looked like he was considering the situation for a moment. His brows furrowed and his mouth twisted. Then he scooted over and flipped onto his side, facing Kate. "We can share! It'll be a tight fit, but I think we can make it work for one night." He patted the covers next to him.

"Well," Kate couldn't see any other option, "okay. If you don't mind." She kicked off her shoes and laid down on the covers beside Kaliq. For a minute, neither of them moved. The bed was only meant for a single person, so contact with the mysterious artist was inevitable. Kate could feel the heat emanating from his skin and her nostrils filled with his scent, which made her think of the forest preserve behind her childhood home. It was familiar and exciting at the same time.

"You know," Kaliq started, kicking off his own shoes, "this kind of reminds me of when my brothers and I would all climb into my oldest brother's bed when we were kids. We'd all squeeze in and stay up all night telling stories about superheroes we made up."

"How many brothers do you have?"

"Four. I'm the second oldest."

"Are they artists too?"

Kaliq's deep laughter filled the tent. "Nooooo, no. Absolutely not. Well, my youngest brother Hamar plays the guitar, but otherwise not a one of them has a single creative bone in his body. My oldest brother is in business, my first younger brother is in law, and my youngest brother is still a student."

"I take it that you weren't exactly encouraged to pursue fine arts?" Kate could tell by the tone of Kaliq's answer that he was accustomed to being the black sheep in his family. She knew that feeling well, being the only girl in her clan who'd almost made it to thirty without a husband, let alone a kid.

"Actually, my parents were huge literature fiends. That's how they met. My father went to study French lit in Paris and my mother was his tutor."

"Oh, so your folks must be pretty well off?" Kate cringed. God, what a dumb thing to ask. She didn't even care about that sort of thing. Her own family was pretty solidly situated in the middle class. She wasn't one of the girls who'd gotten a new car for her sweet sixteen, but she couldn't remember ever really wanting for anything either. Now Kaliq probably thought she was some kind of superficial gold digger.

"Eh," he replied, "I guess you could say that my family is comfortable."

His family may have been comfortable, but he certainly wasn't. Not with that question. Kate changed the subject. "What kind of art do you make?"

This was clearly a more interesting topic to Kaliq. His face lit up. "I'm a painter. I like to do portraits best, of people and animals. Sometimes of people with their pets. I'm pretty old fashioned in that regard. I love figurative art and capturing people's personalities with paint."

"Really? I had you pegged as a sculptor. Maybe someone who worked with metal."

"Why a sculptor?"

"You just seem so macho. It was easy to

imagine you welding or doing some kind of very physical work with huge, minimalist designs. I never would have guessed that you're a sentimental portraitist."

"Hey, for your information, painting is very manly."

"I guess portraits are better than lighthouses or sunsets or something," Kate joked.

"Sometimes I like to put sunsets in the background of my portraits," Kaliq admitted. "But I can assure you that they're always very masculine sunsets. Lots of dramatic reds and oranges."

Kate's metal cot shook as Kaliq laughed from deep in his belly. It really was very hard for her to imagine such a big, tough-looking guy painting pictures of people's cats. "Is there a big demand for traditional portraiture in Samarra?"

"Oh you might be surprised," answered Kaliq as his fingers toyed with the blanket between them. "I've had all sorts of commissions from my parents, my brothers, my aunts, and even some of our closest family friends. If my brothers get married and have families, I may be able to expand my patron base even further." He grinned. "Seriously though, the contemporary art market in Samarra isn't exactly booming. I'd like to go back to New York, but I've got responsibilities to my family here."

"I know that feeling," Kate nodded.

"Really?" Kaliq looked surprised. "You're all the way out here on the other side of the planet leading your own thing. Your parents must be supportive."

"Oh they are," Kate hurried to agree. "I think they're just a little worried about my family situation."

"What is your family situation?"

"That's their concern. I don't have one. All my sisters already have kids."

"Are kids not your thing?"

"Kids are definitely my thing. I'm crazy about 'em. I guess dating is not really my thing."

"Aha," Kaliq looked at the ceiling. "No time for men?"

Kate laughed. "Right. My fast-paced and

glamorous lifestyle digging up giant stone bulls hasn't left any time for romance."

"You need a man who can keep up with you."

"Right now I'd be satisfied with a man who would give me the time of day."

"You must be joking," Kaliq turned to gaze at Kate with his emerald eyes.

Kate snorted. "Sorry. No, I'm not exactly a hot commodity on the dating market back in New York. You know what it's like there. The women are all successful and gorgeous. They're six feet tall and they look like movie stars. There aren't a ton of men looking for a lady with the body of a ten year old boy and a frizzy red afro."

"I like your afro. I think it looks very dignified. Like a lion's mane." Kaliq twirled one of Kate's copper locks around his finger and smiled.

"Shut up," Kate rolled her eyes. She was used to being teased about her hair. She'd learned how to control it, at least insofar as it could be controlled, once she gotten to college. When she was in high school, unfortunately, she really did have a lion's mane. In middle school, she'd been teased relentlessly by her classmates.

"No, really. And you've got those pretty hazel eyes." He brushed his thumb over her cheek, and Kate's pretty hazel eyes nearly bulged out of her head.

Was this guy seriously flirting with her? He was so obviously way, way out of her league. Kaliq was the type of guy who looked like he'd fit right in on the pages of *Men's Vogue* or possibly *Men's Health* when he had his shirt off. He did *not* look like the sort of guy who was interested in Kate. Usually those guys were about half Kaliq's size. And they weren't so charming.

Still, she was pretty sure that Kaliq was putting the moves on her. Kate could feel her heart racing. It had been so long since she's had a date; she didn't want to screw this up. *Act normal, act normal, act normal,* she told herself, trying to prevent some idiotic comment from pouring from her lips.

"So do you want to make out? I mean, we

don't have to if you don't want to. Sorry. I don't know what came over me." Katherine cringed. She couldn't help it. When she got nervous, sometimes her mouth just ran. God, she'd just embarrassed herself in front of the hottest man she'd ever met. She'd probably have to apolo...

Before she knew what was happening, Kaliq's lips were pressed on her own. She opened her mouth and welcomed his tongue inside, greeting it with her own. Holy shit. This was really happening. Kate was kissing the modern-day equivalent of a Greek god.

She wrapped her arms around Kaliq's trunk in an effort to pull him closer. He was so heavy that she ended up pulling herself toward him, but that was just as well. Kate nuzzled up against him and slipped her own tongue into his mouth. He groaned softly and wrapped his arm around her, resting his hand on the small of her back.

Kate was not exactly a shrinking violet when it came to romance, at least not once she knew a guy was for sure interested in her, but she felt like putty in Kaliq's arms. She was still in a state of disbelief over her good luck. After all, it wasn't every day that she found a man like Kaliq by the side of the rode. The way her body was reacting to his attention, though, was very, very real.

She needed more. She wanted to peel Kaliq out of his clothes and see if he really was as gorgeous as she suspected. She could feel the muscle definition in his back and she was dying to feel his warm skin against her own. Kaliq was a phenomenal kisser, and she had no doubt that he knew his way around a woman's body.

Kate pushed him onto his back and climbed aboard. Good grief, he was so thick that she felt like she was straddling a bull instead of a man. She ran her fingers through his shaggy hair and lowered her lips onto his once again. Kaliq nibbled her bottom lip and Kate wiggled in his lap. She could feel him growing hard beneath her and she couldn't help but to imagine the pleasure she was about to experience.

Kaliq's hands moved to her ass and

pulled her in tighter. She could definitely tell at this point that he was turned on. She didn't want to seem too forward, but she was really into the feeling of him pressing up against her. Kate squirmed and whimpered as Kaliq's kiss sent fire through her veins, directly into her panties. Her fingers left Kaliq's hair and set to work on the buttons on the front of her shirt.

"Wait!" Kaliq's strong hands caught Kate by her wrists. "Wait, slow down," he said softly, looking deep into her eyes. "We should slow down. We just met. We don't have to rush into anything."

"Oh," Kate hadn't been expecting this. She didn't think they were moving too fast. Actually, she would have liked to move even faster. She was in the process of moving faster when Kaliq had stopped her. "Okay." She didn't want him to feel pressured to do anything that made him uncomfortable.

She rolled off of him to the side of the bed nearest the wall. Kaliq seemed like a modern guy, but she knew that sex before marriage was still a bit taboo in Samarri society.

"We have all the time in the world, right?" Kaliq stroked Kate's cheek with the back of his fingers. "Or at least six months, while you're digging up those bulls. Let me take you out! You haven't even seen my paintings yet. For all you know, I'm some bum who hangs out by the sides of roads waiting for pretty girls to come by."

Kate had to laugh at that. "Alright, you have a point. You can woo me with your portraits."

"Prepare to be wooed." Kaliq pulled Kate close and wrapped his arms around her. "I bet you've never met a guy like me."

It was true. She hadn't. Something was telling her that she was about to be shown a whole new world.

4

Kate jolted upright in bed. It was still dark in her tent but she could see Kaliq's chest rising and falling with his breath next to her. She had no idea what time it was. It could have been the middle of the night, or dawn could have been approaching. Kaliq was still sound asleep, snoring softly. She laid back down and put her arm around him, snuggling up to his warm body.

She'd had the dream again. Even in the middle of the desert on the other side of the planet, even when she was in bed with the most beautiful man she'd ever met, she couldn't escape it. Katherine sighed and tried to tell herself that she was being silly. That she had no reason to be so insecure.

She couldn't help it though. It didn't seem to matter how much time had passed. The vicious bullying she'd undergone in high school still stung like the wound was fresh. It was dumb, really. Lots of kids got made fun of as teenagers. She certainly hadn't even received the worst of it. It probably wasn't even personal for the kids who bullied her. They probably were more interested in impressing one another than they were in hurting her.

Still. She still cringed about how hurt and humiliated she'd been, and the scenario still played out in her dreams, over and over. When she was a sophomore, right in the midst of her experimental period with makeup and girly dresses, one of the most popular boys in school had asked her to prom.

Kate had been stunned. It made absolutely no sense that this boy wanted to take her to the prom. He'd never noticed her existence.

Even her friends and sisters had been surprised.They reasoned that Kate's new look had caught his eye, and they jumped right in to helping Kate pick a dress and a hair style.

Kate had spent a week preparing for her big date, dreaming about how magical the night would be. She was fifteen, so of course she fantasized about the guy falling in love with her. Her entire life would change. She'd be vaulted into the popular group in school, invited to parties, and adored by fellow students and teachers alike.

When the big day came, her mother helped her to tame her curls into an up-do. She got her makeup done by a professional at a counter in the mall, and she even got her nails painted at a salon. Her dress, which had been a bit of a stretch for her parents' wallets, made her feel like a fairy princess. It was emerald green, fitted in the bodice with a huge, poofy skirt that reached the floor.

For a few hours, between the time she put the dress on and the time she finally admitted to herself that she was being stood up, she was on cloud nine. She'd never felt so beautiful in her life, and she was still grateful to her mother for snapping a few pictures before the night was ruined. The images of her in her parents' garden had hurt too much for her to look at until she was out of college, but she was still glad she had them.

If her mother had photographed the entire night, she could have visually documented Kate's progression from elation to fear to concern to embarrassment to a full-on-hysterical breakdown. When her date still hadn't arrived by nine PM and she knew for sure that he wasn't coming, Katherine had a totally out-of character meltdown. She cried and cried and cried inconsolably until she drifted off to sleep still wearing her green gown.

The next Monday her parents had to practically force her to return to school. All of her friends who had attended the prom had seen her date. He was at the prom with one of the popular girls. Kate had to admit over and over that he hadn't even bothered to tell her that he had another date.

Facing her friends was rough. Facing the guy who stood her up was unthinkable. For the entire week, Kate went out of her way to ensure that she never ran into him. When she finally did run smack into him while rushing from her locker to her AP history class, he laughed at her.

"Hey, Delaney, slow down. You got a hot date? I hope you didn't think I was serious about the prom?"

Kate was dumbstruck. He hadn't given her any indication that he'd been joking when he asked. He had no reason to joke with her like that, especially since they barely knew one another. She just couldn't bring herself to tell him off, though. "Yeah. Yeah, of course. Hilarious."

There was nothing left for her to do but try to preserve whatever little shred of dignity she had left. She pretended like she had realized that the "date" was a joke all along and she never brought it up again. Inside, though, the little prank tore her up.

The worst of it was that she felt like an absolute idiot. Of course a guy like that would never have seriously asked a girl like her to the prom. She was so dumb for thinking that her lame efforts to look more girly had worked. She probably looked like a clown to him and his friends. They'd certainly enjoyed laughing at her.

With time, the sting softened. Every once in a while, though, she'd have the nightmare. She'd wake up in a cold sweat. In her dream, she was actually at the prom in her green dress. Everyone knew that she'd been fooled, and they were all pointing and laughing at her. Sometimes, instead of her fellow high school students, it would be her professors in grad school or her colleagues laughing at her standing there in her green dress.

In this particular iteration of her worst nightmare, it was Kaliq. He was ridiculing her for falling for him, for thinking that a guy as handsome as he was would be interested in a dork like her. He made fun of her dress, her hair, and her boyish figure.

Kate was on the brink of real tears when she woke, but Kaliq's peaceful breathing soothed her. He was really there, in her bed. She didn't know what he was dreaming about, but whatever it was must have been better than what she had been dreaming. She could tell because the faintest smile played at the corners of his lips.

It was too early to get up. It was still pitch black out and there was no reason to risk waking Kaliq from his sweet dreams. Kate held on to him and drifted back off to sleep, this time with thoughts of all the fun they might have dancing around in her head.

When she woke up again a few hours later, she was alone.

"Seriously?" she said out loud to herself, looking around the now-bright tent.

"Hungry?" Kaliq responded, striding through the flap door. "I'm bringing you breakfast in bed. I bet you haven't had that in a while."

"I haven't," Kate agreed, admiring the plate of tray he set on her nightstand. It was plain, the same bread and cheese she ate every day for breakfast plus a French press full of coffee, but she had to admit, it was nice to have someone waiting on her. She felt pampered.

"Did you sleep okay? I'm afraid that I hogged your entire bed."

"I slept fine," Kate lied. "And it's not like you really had any choice; I don't think this bed was made for people your size. I barely fit when I'm alone." She poured herself a nice, hot cup of coffee and layered some cheese on a slice of bread.

"I must have been wiped out from my adventure on the road. I slept like a rock."

"I know," Kate smiled. "How are you feeling today?"

"Like a new man," Kaliq stretched. "So," he took a big swig of his coffee, "are you going to introduce me to Fred and Barney?"

"I'm always ready to introduce interested parties to Fred and Barney," Kate responded, finishing up her own coffee. "Right this way," she led Kaliq out into the bright morning sun.

The camp was already bustling with activity.

Workers were hauling trolleys full of stones and loose earth away from the site, grad students were filling out reports, and Banjo was trotting along at their heels. Work on the lamassu generally went on from sunup to sundown, though they didn't really have a firm schedule.

"Wow," Kaliq admired the giant ten-meter high pair of winged bulls that a dozen or so workers were gently scraping out of the side of a mountain. Each bull had a bearded man's head and an elaborate crown. "I'd heard they were impressive, but I guess it's impossible to capture just how awe-inspiring they are until you see them in real life."

Kate beamed with pride as though she'd sculpted the winged bulls herself. They really were the light of her life. She'd studied them since she was an undergrad and nothing pleased her more than showing them off. "They really are incredible," she agreed. "It's a dream come true for me to be able to work this dig. For a while there, it looked like things weren't going to move forward, what with the border disputes. I'm so, so glad to be here though."

Kate turned to face Kaliq and caught him smirking at her. She cringed a bit. She knew that she had a tendency to nerd out a bit over her job. "Sorry, I just really love ancient culture."

"No, no," Kaliq hurried to respond. "I think it's fantastic that they found someone so passionate to lead this dig. Plus you're right, of course. They're pretty great. I'm glad you're out here revealing them to the world."

Color flooded to Katherine's cheeks. She was determined not to be embarrassed though. She had no reason to believe that Kaliq was being anything other than sincere about his interest in her work. "You want to see the inside?" she volunteered.

"The inside?" Kaliq raised his eyebrows.

"Yeah, there's a series of tunnels in the mountain behind the lamassu. They haven't been completely mapped out yet, so they're not really open to the public, but I can give you an insider's tour. At least a partial tour."

"It's good to have friends in high places,"

joked Kaliq.

"You too can be in a high place if we go in. The tunnels lead up to a lookout point over the bulls. They were probably originally used by the kings' royal guards."

"Hey!" someone interrupted.

Kate looked to see who was approaching and didn't even bother to hide her disdain. It was Jarrod Cole.

"Are you still on your date or did you intend to come to work today?" he sneered.

Kate looked him up and down, taking in his stupid little too-short khaki shorts and his dishwater blond hair. As usual, he was trying to boss her around even though he had absolutely no authority over her. He was probably also trying to make her look bad in front of Kaliq.

Unfortunately for Jarrod, Kate really was not in the mood for his crap. "Did you need help with something?" she answered, trying her best to sound sassy. "Got a rock you need help lifting, maybe?"

"I just thought that, as director of the dig,

you might care about preparing for this afternoon's presentation," Jarrod shot back sauntering away.

Shit. He was right. She had forgotten about the presentation. That afternoon she had to give an update of their progress to the Sheikha Ghazal al Abbas. The Sheikha's organization was funding the entire dig and Kate knew that it was vital to her future that the Sheikha be impressed with her work.

She turned to Kaliq. "Sorry, but could I offer you a rain check on that tour? Cole's an asshole but he's right. We have a presentation this afternoon that I need to prepare."

"No problem," the artist answered. "You nervous?"

"A little."

"I have a feeling," Kaliq smiled mysteriously, "that your big presentation will be a hit."

5

Good, Kate thought, at least that made one person who seemed to have some confidence in her. She helped Kaliq to fill his gas tank with petrol borrowed from the dig's supply tent and watched as he sped off into the distance.

Before he was even out of her sight, he already seemed like a good dream rather than a real person. What had just happened to her? Kate stood watching the road long after he was gone.

"Well," Jarrod startled her from behind.

"I'm glad that you managed to arrange a one-night-stand for yourself even though we're out here working in the middle of the Samarri desert. I hope that I didn't interrupt anything with my little reminder, but I really don't want this project to lose funding. Have you even prepared something to show the Sheikha, or should I take over?"

Kate rolled her eyes, then glared at him. He was standing too close, with one hand on his cargo-shorts-clad hip. "Jesus, Jarrod. Relax. Sorry to disappoint you, but I've had this presentation ready for days. Can you please just go put on some pants? You're dressed like a toddler."

She stormed off back to her tent without waiting for a response. Kate wasn't a nasty person by nature, but Jarrod knew exactly how to push her buttons. She'd tried to make friends with him, then when it was obvious that would never happen, she tried to ignore him. He just wouldn't leave her alone though.

Every day, he sought her out expressly

for the purpose of antagonizing her. He insulted her work, her appearance, her habits, and anything else he could come up with.

Kate didn't even know what his problem was. She'd never done anything to cross him. She always had a smart-ass response ready for him now, but she'd certainly never hurt him on purpose. She guessed that he might be jealous of her very slight authority over him at the dig, but she suspected that it was actually something much deeper. She'd begun to believe that he was just an asshole by nature.

She decided not to let him get her down. That was probably exactly what he wanted, to throw her off her game before her big presentation. God only knows why, since he'd only benefit if she knocked this presentation out of the park.

Katherine shook her curls and headed back to her tent with Banjo. She wanted to shower and put on the only dressy-looking outfit she had, which was a black knee-length dress with a matching jacket. She wasn't quite sure whether the change was necessary, but the dress always made her feel like she looked more mature and polished. It couldn't hurt to have that little self-esteem boost.

She went over her notes, double-checked that her slide presentation was in order, and fussed around with her hair until she was able to get it into a decent French twist. Kate may have been a little unsure of herself when it came to personal interactions, but when it came to the work that she loved, she was in her element. She had no doubt that the Sheikha al Abbas would be impressed by their progress.

Katherine's enthusiasm for her project was her only concern. She knew that she had a tendency to geek out over archaeological subjects, and she had no idea how much detail the Sheikha was interested in hearing. The Sheikha founded and directed the Samarri cultural preservation organization that funded most of the dig, so presumably she was at least somewhat interested in the lamassu, but Kate wasn't sure if she was a hardcore artifact nut or just a very generous woman.

Kate slipped into her black high heels, which really only had about an inch of heel, and wobbled down to the big tent they used for meals and meetings. Mike already had everything set up for her, including a big white projection screen and several bottles of water for everyone attending the meeting.

"You all set, boss?" he asked her, taking the seat next to her.

"You know there's nothing I love better than a captive audience," she joked.

"Speaking of a captive, I guess you and that guy you found hit it off, eh? He seems like a cool dude."

Kate felt the color rise in her cheeks. She couldn't help it; it was one of the drawbacks of being a natural redhead. "Yeah, he was really nice. He's an artist here. Does portraits."

"Maybe he'll do a portrait of you. That would be rad. Man, Jarrod was *pissed*. He spent the entire night bitching about how you were causing a security risk and being unprofessional. He said some really nasty stuff."

Kate rolled her eyes. "What the hell is that guy's problem?"

Mike looked surprised. "He's obviously into you. Don't worry. Everyone could tell how jealous he was, and no one listened to his bullshit."

"I don't think so," Kate scrunched up her face and shook her head. "I think he really, honest-to-God hates me, and I have no idea why."

"Trust me," Mike nodded. "The guy digs you. He just doesn't know how to deal with it without being a douchecanoe."

Kate didn't think Mike was right, but she didn't have time to argue. People were pouring into the tent and taking their seats. Sheikha al Abbas and her entourage were due to arrive any moment.

She could hear some kind of commotion outside and she correctly assumed that it was the Sheikha arriving. The roar of engines reached her ears and confirmed that it was show time. Kate smoothed her hair back and took a deep breath.

"So as you can see," she heard Jarrod's high nasally voice before she saw him open the door to the tent, "we've made quite a bit of progress. I think you're going to be pleased." Jeez, was that guy even capable of saying anything out loud without sounding like a complete ass?

In stepped the most elegant lady Kate had seen since she had arrived in Samarra. Not only the most elegant, but also the tiniest. Kate was surprised to see that the top of Sheikha al Abbas's teased bangs definitely didn't reach five feet. It was rare that Kate met an adult smaller than herself and she immediately liked the woman.

The Sheikha was dressed in an ivory, floor-length, fitted dress with a matching sport coat and a silk turban wrapped around her head. She wore huge, black sunglasses that hid her face and even from across the room, Kate could see gold dripping from her ears, wrists, and neck.

Katherine didn't think she'd ever met such a fancy lady. She stood and extended her hand to the Sheikha, not entirely sure of what the proper way to greet the woman would be. "Sheikha al Abbas, welcome. Thank you so much for agreeing to meet with us today, and thank you for your continued support. We wouldn't be able to preserve the lamassu without your interest."

The tiny woman took Kate's hand and smiled while removing her sunglasses to reveal her perfectly made-up face. "Please, call me Ghazal." Kate admired Ghazal's flawless skin. With her matte red lipstick and black liquid eyeliner, she kind of reminded Kate of the desert version of a classic movie starlet. She really couldn't tell how old the other woman was. The Sheikha didn't have a visible wrinkle on her face, but she still somehow looked wise and experienced. She really could have been either forty or sixty and Kate wouldn't have been surprised.

"Please," Kate indicated the best seat at the table, which was a metal folding chair, but at least it was the least wobbly chair, "we'd love to show you how far we've come." Kate had gone over her presentation so many times that she didn't even really need her notes.

"Oh," Ghazal cringed. "I thought perhaps we could tour the site."

"Of course," Kate quickly replied. "I'll just get

you up to date on our work and then we can head outside."

"Sweetheart," Ghazal smiled, "would you be terribly disappointed if we skipped the presentation? I'd really love to see these bulls I've been hearing so much about and I was never a very good student."

"Sure," Kate was surprised. She had been certain that the Sheikha would want to know exactly what her money was going toward. "Sure, we can get right out to the dig."

"I'm so glad you understand. I'm sure that you and Dr. Cole have done an outstanding job with your reports and such. I probably wouldn't really have understood them anyways. I must confess; I love ancient art but I'm actually not very informed about things like soil composition and all of this chemistry stuff that Dr. Cole was talking about."

"Ah" Kate understood. "Jarrod loves to talk rocks. I'm not surprised you've had enough lecturing."

"Oh, it wasn't so bad," Ghazal laughed.

"Besides, I already know all I need to know about the two of you. I can never repay you for what you did for my son."

Kate's face blanched. "Excuse me?" she managed to peep out.

"Well, technically he is my husband's son, but I've always considered Kaliq like a son." Ghazal added, as though that info clarified anything. "Oh yes, we've already heard all about how you came to his rescue when he was stranded out there. My word, we've been nagging him about that old motorcycle for years. He could have died out there if you hadn't come by in the nick of time!"

Kate felt like she was going to throw up. "Your son?" she whispered. Her head was spinning and she knew that she needed to get a hold of herself before she embarrassed herself, but she'd been completely blindsided.

She could see Jarrod trying to get her attention from the corner of her eye, but Kate knew that she just didn't have the wherewithal to deal with whatever bullshit he was trying to serve up. If Kaliq was the Sheikha al Abbas's son, that made him one of the four Sheikhs al Abbas.

Everyone who knew anything at all about Samarri culture knew about the al Abbas brothers. Their family was literally local royalty, and they didn't rule Samarra directly, but they were certainly the most powerful men in the country. Actually, they were some of the most powerful men in the entire region. Each brother was worth at least a billion dollars and Kate was a moron for not recognizing Kaliq's name.

Why the hell had he lied to her? Kate didn't even know how to feel. She never would have hopped into bed with him if she had known who he really was. She needed to maintain a professional relationship with the al Abbas family, or she'd risk losing their funding for the dig. Dozens of people would be unemployed if Sheikha Ghazal decided to pull her support for any reason.

Plus, Kate felt like an absolute fool for daydreaming about having any kind of relationship with Kaliq. Men in positions like his didn't date women in positions like hers, let alone get into serious relationships with them. There was no way that he'd ever be her boyfriend.

Kate had to admit that Kaliq hadn't exactly mislead her on that front, though. He'd never said that he was going to be her boyfriend. It was her own fault that she'd let her overactive imagination run away with dreams of moving into a loft with him where she could have a huge collection of first edition histories of texts on ancient art and he could have a space that served as his painting studio.

There was nothing for Kate to do but swallow her feelings and lead the Sheikha on her tour. She'd just have to hope that Kaliq hadn't shared every detail of his rescue. She gathered her things, led the Sheikha and her security detail out into the bright midday sun, and resolved to forget that she had ever met Kaliq.

6

"They're fabulous," Ghazal al Abbas gushed, sweeping her arm towards the lamassu. "I can't believe I've lived in Samarra for nearly my entire life and I've never seen these in person. You're really doing outstanding work here."

Kate couldn't help but to flush with pride, as though the Sheikha's comment was personal and directed at her. "They really are awe-inspiring," she agreed with the older woman. If there was one thing that could always raise her spirits, it was her work. Kate was lucky to have found her calling and she always appreciated it when people admired the things that she loved.

Ghazal was shockingly disarming and easy to befriend. Despite her glamorous looks, she was very down-to-earth and even funny. She joked about how her girlhood dreams of being a sculptor had never panned out and told Kate about her assorted projects, including her cultural foundation and several schools she had funded for disadvantaged local children.

"You know," she added, following Kate back to the main tent, "my husband was also a creative soul. That's how he met Kaliq's mother, his first wife. He was studying literature in Paris. That's where our Kaliq gets it, his urge to paint. It's in his blood."

So Kaliq wasn't a total liar, Kate thought to herself. Still, she was angry about feeling duped by the Sheikh and was glad she'd never have to see him again. She was dreading the inevitable lecture from Jarrod but, the longer the shock had to set in, the less terrible it seemed. She had even begun to think of reasons why Kaliq might not have mentioned his Sheikh-hood.

"So," Ghazal faced Kate once they were back at the tent. "I've arranged a little surprise for you. A gift to thank you and your team for the excellent work you've done, and also to thank you for saving my son's life."

"Oh!" Kate glanced up to the Sheikha, "that's not necessary! We're the ones who should be thanking you. You've made all this possible."

"Of course it's not necessary," Ghazal responded. "I want to treat you. I've arranged for a little party tonight. Please bring your entire staff and join my family at my son Amir's home. We've arranged a lovely traditional Samarri dinner and there will be music and dancing. I'm looking forward to introducing you to the rest of my family. My driver can leave instructions about how to reach us. Please come by at six and we can celebrate together." Ghazal took Kate's face in her hands and kissed each cheek before floating off with her bevy of dark-suited security guards.

Shit. Shit, shit shit. This was bad. Kate couldn't very well tell the Sheikha that she wasn't going to attend her party. It was an incredibly generous gesture, and Kate knew that she absolutely had to be there. She also knew, without a doubt, that Kaliq would be there.

The one thing she wasn't sure about was how she was going to avoid him. She was sure that Ghazal had sprung this party on him just like she'd sprung it on Kate. There was no way that he would want to see Kate after their almost-one-night-stand.

Kate tried to comfort herself with the assumption that Kaliq would probably want to avoid her even more than she wanted to avoid him. She'd just go to the party, make polite conversation with the other members of the al Abbas family, then leave as early as possible. She definitely wouldn't get drunk and she wouldn't have any kind of private talk with Kaliq.

For the time being, her biggest concern

would be avoiding Jarrod. Kate knew that he'd probably be lurking in the tent, waiting to pounce on her. She wanted to collect her notes, but the instinct to flee her coworker was stronger, so she just strode right back to her own tent. She could get her stuff later.

Kate wished that she had something a little dressier to wear to this party. Her Samarri wardrobe consisted of jeans, tank tops, white men's shirts, and the one dress suit she already had on. She'd just have to wear the dress without the jacket to the party. If she had time, she could have run down to the market and picked up a kaftan. There were several she had her eye on, and it had long been her intention to bring some home for herself, her mother, and her sisters. She hadn't pulled the trigger yet on buying them because she hadn't realized that she'd have an occasion to wear one while still in Samarra.

At least she had the dress she was wearing. She also had a pair of amethyst stud earrings that her father had given her for graduating with her doctorate. Kate wore them all the time, regardless of how formal her plans were, but they gave her a boost of confidence nevertheless. As a freckled redhead, dark purple and forest green were the only colors that really flattered her.

Kate checked her watch. She had about two hours to kill before she'd need to head out. She knew that she probably shouldn't stay in her tent if she wanted to avoid Jarrod; once he figured out that she wasn't returning to the big tent, he'd probably check her quarters next.

Kate slipped out of her tent and headed to Mike's. He was her best friend on-site and Jarrod seemed slightly intimidated by him. Kate didn't know whether it was because Mike was kind of a big guy or whether it might be because Mike seemed totally oblivious to Jarrod's passive-aggressive snips, but Jarrod tended to avoid Mike, which made his tent one of the most appealing in Samarra.

"Knock knock," she said softly outside the flap to Mike's tent. She didn't want to barge in on him, but you couldn't exactly knock on a tent door. "Mike? You in there?"

"Boss?" she heard him call back. "That you?"

"Yeah. You busy?"

"No," Mike peeked his blond head out. "Come in."

Kate entered Mike's very messy tent. He had laundry and books all over the floor and there were a couple of dirty plates on his card table.

"Sorry for the mess," Mike noticed her checking out his dishes. "I wasn't expecting anyone or I would have cleaned up."

"Don't worry about it," Kate answered, taking a seat in one of Mike's folding chairs. "My tent doesn't look much better."

"So I guess you knocked it out of the park with the Sheikha? With the entire al Abbas family from what I hear," grinned Mike. "They're throwing some kind of banquet in your honor now? Nice work," he laughed.

Kate smirked and rolled her eyes. "I don't think it was my charm so much as the lamassu that impressed her."

"Are you excited to see your new dude tonight?"

Kate cringed. "He's not really my new dude."

"Really? Wow. I would have thought that a dude like that could get any woman he wanted. You holding out for a king? Good thinking. This guy probably only has like a billion bucks. You don't want to sell yourself short."

Kate knew that Mike was just kidding, but she was still a little annoyed. She toyed with a napkin on his table, gazing down at her shoes.

"Hey, I didn't mean to say anything dumb," Mike looked worried. "I was just joking around a little."

"Oh, it's not you," Kate finally admitted. "I just feel like an idiot. Kaliq didn't tell me who he was. God, it sounds so dumb now, but I assumed that he was just an ordinary guy and he never told me otherwise. He didn't exactly lie, but he wasn't honest and now I feel like I was duped."

"You mean he didn't tell you he was a

Sheikh?" Mike's eyebrows went up. "I wonder why he'd hide that."

"I have no idea," she really didn't.

"Maybe it just didn't come up? Like, he didn't see a good time to insert 'by the way, I'm kind of a big deal' into whatever conversation you guys were having?"

"But he told me all about his family and how he wanted to be a painter but he couldn't ditch his responsibilities. He just didn't specify what those responsibilities were."

"Huh," Mike replied. "In that case, I don't know what this guy's deal is. Are you gonna talk to him about it?"

"No way," Kate shook her head. "What would I even say? I'm just gonna avoid him and pretend like nothing happened."

"Did you guys...?"

"No," Kate shook her head. "I kind of wanted to though. Now I'm glad we didn't. I wouldn't want things to get weird with his family."

"If things got weird, it would be his fault.

You're right, though, you'd probably be the one who had to deal with the consequences. Are you bummed?"

"Kind of. I'm mostly disappointed and embarrassed. I *really* don't want to have any sort of conversation at all about this with Jarrod, but I'm sure he can't wait to dig into me."

"Don't worry about that guy," Mike shook his head. "Everyone knows he's a tool. The grad students all hate him. I'm sure he'll probably try to give you shit, but you should just ignore him. If you want, we can ride to this party together. Dr. Cole usually avoids me."

"Thanks Mike. Do you mind if we just kind of show up and then leave early? I don't really want to have any awkward conversations with Sheikh Kaliq either. I'd rather just show up, thank the Sheikha, and disappear as soon as I can."

"Yeah, I don't mind. As long as I can eat enough lamb to feed a small army while we're there. I heard there's gonna be a buffet."

"Oh, you have my word. I'll match you

kebab for kebab. I'm sick of peanut butter sandwiches too." Technically they had a cook at their site, but there were only so many ways to prepare lentils and rice. Both lunch and dinner tasted the same every day, and most of the archaeologists were living on stockpiles of peanut butter, Nutella, chips, and Snickers bars that could be bought at the local market.

The Samarri food was tasty and Kate always made it a point to try something new when she visited the market. She might not have been looking forward to the socializing that the party would require, but she was definitely looking forward to the banquet. She was a small girl, but she didn't have a small appetite. Her game plan for this banquet was to arrive, load up her plate, say hello to the Sheikha and any relative she wanted to introduce, then head back to the camp in time to watch a movie on her laptop before bed.

"So," Mike started, "mind if I get changed? We can meet at the truck in half an hour."

"Oh!" Kate hadn't realized that she was holding him up. "Sure. Half an hour. See you there."

Kate made her way out of Mike's tent and slinked back to Fred and Barney, taking care to avoid the camp's main thoroughfares. She only needed to evade Jarrod for a while longer, and she knew the perfect spot.

She slipped behind Fred and entered the cave that led through the mountain and back upward to a ledge near the bull's head. Dr. Cole very rarely entered the caves; they hadn't been declared safe by the engineers yet and he was afraid they'd collapse on him. Kate had been through several tunnels, though, and they looked okay to her. She loved exploring them, and she especially loved climbing to the lookout platform at the top.

After a brief climb, she peeked out onto the ledge. She could see her own tent from where she was standing and, sure enough, there was Jarrod Cole parked outside of her door. Well, she thought, that was just fine with her. He could go ahead and wait all night.

7

The remainder of the afternoon fled by. Kate waited until the last moment, then made her way quickly from her secret ledge to the truck where she would meet Mike. He was showered and ready to go, so they sped off into the desert without waiting to greet anyone else.

The party was held at Amir al Abbas'

desert villa. It was slightly over an hour away from the dig site and Kate and Mike rode together in the truck, listening to the classic rock he liked to play on the truck's cassette deck. That was one of the things Kate liked about Mike; they felt comfortable not talking for long stretches.

Once they arrived at the villa, both of them were blown away by it's size and trappings. They had to be buzzed in at the gate, and once they were past the giant, wrought iron doors, it was like they had suddenly driven into Hollywood. Kate could see a bubbling fountain surrounded by a driveway already packed with luxury SUVs. A Spanish colonial style home was framed with bougainvillea that Kate suspected was imported.

"Wow," Mike said what she was thinking out loud. "They really are loaded."

Kate wondered whether Kaliq lived in a similar home. Did he have servants waiting on him hand and foot? Had he ever flown commercial? Even if he wasn't living quite as large as his oldest brother, he was far from the struggling artist he'd led her to believe he was.

"You ready?" Mike parked the truck behind a shiny black Land Rover.

"Ready as I'll ever be," Kate responded, deciding then and there that she wasn't going to spend the entire night moping about how Kaliq had led her on. She hopped out of Mike's truck and made her way up the stairs to the double front doors, which were wide open. They could hear people talking and laughing inside, and Kate could already smell the cinnamon that was so popular with Samarri chefs.

"Mmm," Mike sniffed the air. "Should we find the food?"

"Actually," Kate tilted her head, "I could use a drink. You think they're serving booze?"

"I hope so," Mike peered inside the open door. They stepped into the foyer and were greeted by several of their own coworkers, holding plates of finger food and glass flutes filled with champagne.

Kate glanced around the room and spotted a young man holding a tray of full glasses. She caught him and grabbed a flute for herself and another for Mike. She would have preferred beer, but she was grateful for any small relief to her anxiety. She gulped down her glass and grabbed another before the guy could drift off.

Kaliq was nowhere to be seen. Kate couldn't spot Jarrod either. She began to relax a bit and split off from Mike so that he could chat with some of the other grad students.

"Kate?" she heard Sheikha Ghazal calling her and turned to see the Sheikha dressed like she was ready to attend the Samarri version of the Academy Awards. The lady was wearing a long black evening gown and a heavy collar made of intricate gold leaves. She also wore her makeup and hair differently than she had in the afternoon. Her eyes were smoky now and her long hair cascaded down her back. It was a mystery to Kate how she'd achieved this new look so quickly.

"Have you got something to drink? Wonderful. I'm so glad you could make it. You look fantastic." The Sheikha introduced Kate to an array of family members, including her husband's other wives and a great number of aunties, cousins, and siblings. Every woman Kate met looked like a movie star.

All of them except for Amir's wife, who looked like an ordinary, yet exhausted pregnant suburban wife from Texas. This lady was big and blonde and had a cute southern drawl. She and Kaliq's brother were expecting their first child any day. Kate had been surprised by the woman's appearance at first. She didn't fit in with the rest of the women at the party. She soon learned, however, that this pregnant blonde was some kind of big deal doctor who directed all of Samarra's public health clinics.

Kate assumed that the lady was from some wealthy oil family back in Texas and that was how she'd met her Sheikh husband. She probably looked considerably more glamorous when she wasn't moments away from giving birth. The lady, whose name was Michelle, was actually very down to Earth and friendly.

"So you're leading the dig on those giant

winged bull things?" she'd asked Kate, leaning against a table for support.

"Do you want to sit down?"

"If you don't mind." The ladies took a corner of a big leather sofa.

"My sisters all have kids, but I'm kind of the black sheep. Have you been out to see the lamassu?"

"I haven't been out much at all lately. I mostly just eat and sleep. I've seen pictures though. Kaliq says they're incredible."

Just the sound of Kaliq's name made Kate freeze up. She had no idea what he'd told his family about her, and she didn't particularly want to find out. "I'm sorry, can you excuse me for one moment? I need to use the ladies' room."

"Oh, no problem," Kaliq's sister-in-law answered. "Just go out that door to the back, head down the covered archway, and take the door to the right."

Kate followed the other woman's instructions, making her way through the throngs, past several life-size paintings of horses, and into a fragrant courtyard. She could see men and women setting up long tables full of food and she thanked God that the night was progressing quickly. She and Mike could just eat and run, and she wouldn't have to confront Jarrod or Kaliq.

She was so interested in the dishes being laid out that she didn't notice the hulking form lumbering down the walkway toward her. She ran right smack into a broad, solid wall of a man.

"Excuse me," she tried to skirt around the man but a strong arm slipped around her waist. Kate kept her eyes on the ground in front of her. She didn't need to look up. She knew who it was. She recognized his cologne, that woodsy blend that reminded her of her home.

"Whoa," Kaliq tightened his grip as Kate tried to escape. "Kate?"

"Excuse me, *Sheikh al Abbas*, I was just trying to find the ladies' room."

"Sheikh? Kate, what's going on? It's me, Kaliq."

Of course Kate had recognized Kaliq right away, though he did look quite different than he had when she had rescued him. His glossy hair was pulled back into a ponytail and he was wearing a tailored suit that even she could tell was expensive. He also looked much healthier than he had when he was dehydrated in her tent. His cheeks were flushed and his skin was smooth and more youthful looking.

Kate had hoped that she wouldn't have to speak to Kaliq at the party, but instead she had literally run right into him. There was no avoiding him now; his arm was practically a small tree trunk.

She had no idea what to say though. She wanted to call him a liar, but technically he hadn't told any lies. Plus she couldn't say anything that would put his family's support at risk. Kate gave Kaliq an exasperated sigh. "Sheikh al Abbas, I don't think this is appropriate considering your family's relationship to my work."

Now it was Kaliq's turn to roll his eyes and sigh. "I see. What is it, exactly, that you find inappropriate?"

He still hadn't removed his arm from Kate's waist. In fact, he had pulled her so close that she could feel his breath on her neck as he spoke. Kate tried to turn her head from him but his massive frame was impossible for her to ignore. "Kaliq..."

"Is it this?" he asked, pulling her face towards his and pressing his lips to her own. "Is this what you found inappropriate?"

"Stop," she turned her head again. Kate knew that she couldn't resist him for long. "Stop! I'm sorry, but I'm not interested in a one-night-stand."

"Who said anything about a one-night-stand? I've been looking forward to seeing you again all day."

Kate wriggled against Kaliq but he didn't release her. "Please. We both know that someone like you would never date someone like me. Otherwise you wouldn't have hidden your true identity."

"I didn't hide anything!"

"You just didn't think it was relevant? You

didn't think you ought to tell me that you were on your way to the site to scout things out for your mother's foundation? That just slipped your mind?"

Kaliq groaned. "Okay. Maybe I didn't come completely clean. It wasn't because I was trying to trick you though."

"Oh? What was it then?" Kate genuinely had no idea why else Kaliq would have hidden his position from her. It's not as though she had any kind of interest in Samarri politics.

"Kate, it's not always fun to be a Sheikh. It's a lot of responsibility and it affects every single personal interaction I have. I just wanted to be an ordinary man for a day. I was flattered by the way you seemed to like me just for me rather than for my family name. I made a mistake and I apologize."

"Wait, you lied to me because you thought that I would be powerless to resist you if I knew you were a big deal?" Actually, Kate had been powerless to resist him because he was hot, but still. She didn't like his insinuation.

"You don't understand what it's like."

"I'm sure I don't. I'm just an ordinary working stiff, much like you told me you were. I don't know anything about the problems faced by royalty. Apparently you don't want me to know anything about the problems faced by royalty. That's fine. I'll just be on my way."

"You aren't being fair and I won't allow you to walk away from me."

"Sorry, Sheikh, I don't belong to you. I'm free to walk where I please." Kate made another effort to leave, but Kaliq wouldn't release her.

"You don't seem very free to me right now. Stop resisting me. You're being ridiculous."

This wasn't the Kaliq that Kate thought she knew. This wasn't the same easygoing man who stayed up all night with her chatting about his dreams of becoming a painter. This new Kaliq was intimidating in an entirely new way. He looked like some kind of business man in his suit. Suits had always made Kate nervous, they struck her as authoritarian, and with his hair pulled back his cheekbones looked far more sharp and angular.

He was still handsome, but he seemed even further out of her reach. Kaliq looked like a man who attended important meetings and was accustomed to getting his way. Kate was angry and shocked by his behavior, but she was more shocked by how badly she had misjudged his character. He wasn't a nice person at all, and in fact, the longer he held her, the more she felt like he was possibly dangerous.

"Kaliq, I'm serious, you're making me very uncomfortable right now and if you don't let me go, I'll scream for help."

Kaliq looked down into Kate's eyes. He must have seen that she was genuinely frightened, and the smirk left his face. His grip loosened and Kate took a step back so that she was no longer making contact with him.

"I thought that things could be different between us," he said softly, his dark green eyes reflecting the candlelight that lined the archway.

Kate had no response to that. It didn't matter to her how accustomed he was to getting his way; she wasn't going to let him use her like that. She fled down the dark red tiles into the darkness of Amir's brother's home. She needed to be alone for a second, if only to gather her wits. She couldn't trust herself around Kaliq any longer.

8

"Are you sure about that?" Mike raised his eyebrow as Kate grabbed yet another flute of champagne. "You didn't have much to eat."

"I'm very thirsty," Kate replied, taking a big gulp. Champagne normally gave her a headache, but she needed the distraction that a few drinks would bring and there was no beer available. "What?" she asked when Mike made a face. "It's hot."

It was true, it was an especially warm evening, even for the desert. Or at least it seemed hot. Kate could feel that her cheeks were rosy and she wished that she was wearing one of the loose, flowing dresses that some of the Samarri ladies had on instead of her more structured cocktail dress.

She and Mike were sitting in a pair of iron garden chairs the courtyard in proximity to the buffet. Mike was on his third plate of grilled meats, but Kate had lost her appetite. She didn't think she could handle a heavy meal with her nerves in the condition they were in after she escaped from Kaliq's clutches. Plus, Kaliq had been staring at her from across the courtyard for the entire night. He hadn't bothered her again, but he was watching her every move and giving Mike some serious stink eye.

Fortunately Mike seemed totally oblivious to the extra attention. His focus remained on his food and the conversation they were having about his girlfriend back home. He planned to ask her to be his wife as soon as his time at the dig was up and he was soliciting Kate's opinions on big, public proposals.

"So if you were Mel, you wouldn't want to be surprised in front of a crowd?"

"Of strangers? I definitely wouldn't. I would probably be terrified. I don't really like to be put on the spot though. Some women do. You know Melanie better than I do, so you'd know what she likes."

Kate was having a tough time following Mike. They'd had the same conversation at least a hundred times. Mike was vacillating back and forth between planning a big public spectacle of a proposal and a quiet, intimate dinner proposal. Kate was in favor of the private proposal, but she had actually never met Melanie, so she couldn't say for sure what she thought the other woman would most appreciate.

It took all of her willpower not to look over at Kaliq, who was pretending to have a conversation with a younger man who resembled him but had shorter hair on the other side of the room. Kate could see him peering over at her from the corner of her eye and his own green eyes were like a magnet for hers. She wanted to stare back so badly, but she wanted to preserve what little scrap of dignity she was hanging on to even more.

"What would be your ideal proposal?"

"Me?" Kate was startled. She had actually never considered how she wanted to be proposed to. She'd thought an awful lot about what it would be like to have a husband and children, but she hadn't put too much thought to the actual milestone moments like the proposal or the wedding. "Hmm. Well, I guess I would like a totally private proposal in a romantic spot. Maybe some place that had some personal significance to my proposer and I? That would be sweet."

Kate had never really been one for grand romantic gestures. Then again, she'd never dated anyone who had performed any grand romantic gestures. She didn't know for sure whether she'd be flattered, impressed, or uncomfortable. Maybe all three.

It's not like it mattered at the moment. For the time being, she couldn't even find a normal guy who was willing to date her. Forget romantic gestures; she just wanted someone to call her own. Unfortunately, she'd been a complete failure in that regard. Regular guys just weren't interested in her. She looked kind of weird, and if they weren't turned off by her frizzy red hair, they were turned off by her lack of social skills.

When it came to being just friends, men couldn't get enough of Kate. They considered her one of the guys, except sometimes they'd ask her advice about their girlfriends, much like Mike was doing that very moment. She'd heard men claim that she was like their little sister, sometimes they said she was like their big sister, sometimes they'd even say she was a bro. No one ever said she was hot though.

Then, the one time a man did seem to be interested in her, he turned out to be playing some kind of game with her. Kate finished her drink and turned her attention back to Mike. He was describing a park where he'd once taken his girlfriend on a date. Normally Kate was perfectly content to listen to Mike chatting about how happy he was, but the champagne had gone to her head a bit and Kaliq was still making her uncomfortable from across the room.

"Mike, sorry to interrupt, but I need to use the ladies again," Kate excused herself. She stood up from the chair where she'd been sitting and her head spun a little. She steadied herself on the chair's back and made her way back into the dark archway that surrounded the courtyard.

She and Mike had stayed much later than they had planned. Jarrod, for reasons unknown to anyone, hadn't even shown up at the party. That meant that nearly everyone who worked the site was having a much more pleasant night than expected. People were standing around, sipping champagne, and enjoying the warm evening and delicious food. No one was in a hurry to leave, and since Kaliq had decided to leave Kate alone after their first encounter, she didn't want to make Mike take her back.

Kate didn't actually need to use the restroom. She just wanted a moment alone. Now that she was up, her curiosity was getting the better of her. The archway was lined with solid wood doors and she was dying to see what was behind them, but there was no way she could open one without attracting attention.

She slipped along the dark tile like a cat, peeking around the courtyard and down hallways. Kaliq had disappeared. He must have either gotten tired of glaring at her or maybe gone to the bathroom himself. Kate could still see the Sheikha Ghazal, talking with a pair of ladies around her age. One was tall and severe looking, the other plump and grandmotherly. She could also see the al Abbas family's servants relaxing in the shadows.

The courtyard really was a gorgeous space. There was a huge fountain in the center, filling the night air with the peaceful sound of trickling water. So many citrus trees and exotic flowers occupied pots dotted throughout the yard that Kate felt like she was in an actual garden. The plants' fragrance mingled with the scent of spices and the warm desert breeze.

This may have been the most glamorous party Kate had ever attended. She guessed that it was a relatively casual affair for the al Abbas family, thrown together at the last second, but the house alone was more luxurious than any place Kate had ever been. What was basically the equivalent to a backyard barbecue to Kaliq's family was fancier that Kate's sisters' weddings had been.

Kate really, really, really wanted to see the rest of the inside of the house. She didn't know if it was because it was the coolest private residence she'd ever seen, or because she was kind of drunk, but she felt like she absolutely had to take a little tour.

Too bad things had gone sideways with Kaliq. If he had just been honest with her when they met, she wouldn't have had her teeny bopper make-out session with him and they could have been on friendly terms. Their relationship would have been strictly professional, but friendly. She could have just asked him for a tour.

As it stood, though, the only way she was going to get a tour of Kaliq's brother's sweet mansion was if she led that tour herself. She had made her way to the end of the archway and could see a pair of big wooden doors at the short end of the courtyard. They matched the big wooden doors that led to the front room she had passed through on the way in.

Kate glanced around the courtyard. She was hidden in the shadows and hadn't attracted any attention. Most of the party guests, al Abbas friends and family members and archaeologists alike, were busy chatting away in small groups or picking at the buffet. Many of them were probably just as deep in their cups as Kate was.

She decided to go for it. She slipped down the short walk to the door and tried the handle. It was open. Kate let herself into the dark room on the other side and closed the door behind her as quickly as she could without making a sound.

It took several moments for Kate's eyesight to acclimate to the new environment. She could tell she was in a big, airy room with high ceilings. The walls were decorated with giant works of art, and Kate could make out furniture in the room. Once she got used to the darkness, she realized that the room she was in was very, very similar to the room she had been welcomed into on the other side of the courtyard.

Well. That was a slight disappointment. Kate approached the artwork on the walls. There were four giant paintings in total, each picturing a running horse. She looked closely at the work and determined that it was a different horse in each work. One had a thick white stripe down his nose, while the next had just a star on his forehead. They were portraits. Now this was interesting.

She ran her fingers over the surface of one of the paintings. From far away, the picture looked like it might be a photograph. It was so realistic. From up close, though, she could see that the paint was actually applied very thickly. She could feel ridges and dips.

Kate was absolutely sure that Kaliq had painted these horse portraits. She wondered how long they had taken to complete. They were nearly life sized. Either Kaliq's brother or his wife must have been a real horse nut, considering the prominence the portraits took in their home. Kate wondered if Kaliq was an equestrian enthusiast too, or whether he just liked painting them.

"So you're trying to make it a two night stand?"

Kate squeezed her eyes shut. She knew that voice. "Jarrod. How lovely. For a minute there, I thought you'd decided not to attend."

"My ride left without me. I had to wait for the night guards to arrive. They dropped me off."

Jarrod was a grown man, well into his thirties, but he didn't drive. Kate had offered to teach him when she first arrived at the site, before she realized that he was a raging asshole, but he preferred to be chauffeured around.

Usually the grad students were stuck with the task, but they must have snuck off without him. Kate certainly couldn't blame them.

"So are you waiting for him?"   Kate didn't even bother pretending not to know who Jarrod was talking about. "I'm not waiting for anyone."

Jarrod snorted. "He wasn't interested in a second round, eh? Well Kate, you can't really be too surprised. You're a big girl. You must have known that a man like Sheikh al Abbas couldn't possibly have anything more than a fleeting fancy in a girl like you. Probably doesn't meet too many redheads out here, I bet that was novel for him."

Kate glared at Jarrod and wished she had a drink to throw at him. He responded by pulling a sad face. "Aw, I hope I didn't hurt your feelings."

He was standing so close that Kate could smell his sour breath. She tried to take a step back, but she stumbled over an end table and Jarrod grabbed her to prevent her from falling on her butt. "Whoa there," his face was way too close to hers for comfort, "are you drunk?"

"Jarrod, let me go." Kate was leaning back as far as she possibly could in order to avoid Jarrod's disgusting breath. He didn't release his grip though. "Damn it Jarrod, this isn't funny. Stop."

"Come on, Kate," Jarrod hissed. "We both know that you're not going to get what you want. Not from the Sheikh, at least. That doesn't mean we can't have a little fun. Quit playing hard to get. It's not cute."

At this point, Kate had to crane her neck to get her face away from Jarrod's. She had no idea what the hell he thought he was doing, but she had to get out of their, preferably without attracting any attention or making a scene.

9

"She said she's not interested," a deeper voice boomed from the darkness.

Both Kate and Jarrod were startled. Kate craned her neck around and saw a huge, hulking form in the shadows. The voice was familiar to her, but she couldn't be absolutely certain. Even if she was wrong about who it was, she was grateful for the intervention.

"Look," Jarrod didn't even loosen his grip on Kate, "you have no idea what you just walked in on. Mind your own business. Just go back to grilling kebabs or whatever it is you're supposed to be doing right now."

"Oh I think the kebabs can wait a minute." Kaliq emerged from the darkness and grabbed Jarrod by the back of his collar, pulling him off of Kate and throwing him to the ground.

"Sheikh al Abbas!" Jarrod practically screamed as he went down. "There was no need to assault me! My God," He stayed on the floor and backed away in a sort of crab walk as though Kaliq was still threatening him even though the bigger man hadn't moved. "You could have seriously injured me." Jarrod straightened out his clothes and looked himself over as if checking for injuries. Judging by the way he was behaving, you'd think that Kaliq had thrown him out of a third story window rather than just onto the floor.

Jarrod was being so ridiculous, in fact,

that Kate was having a hard time suppressing her laughter. "Give it a rest, Jarrod," she offered her hand to help him up to his feet, but he ignored her.

"Don't come any closer!" Jarrod shrieked back. "I'm calling the police and filing charges. Don't think that just because you're rich you can get away with attacking innocent people."

"I didn't attack you," Kaliq replied, his deep voice ominous, "If I had attacked you, you wouldn't be squealing at me like an angry pig right now. And please, go ahead and contact the police. Tell them exactly what happened. Did you know that the punishment for sexual assault in Samarra is death?"

"Sexual assault?" cried Jarrod. "Kate and I were having a private moment before you interrupted us."

"No we weren't," Kate interjected. "You were manhandling me."

"Oh please," Jarrod finally turned his attention to Kate. "You obviously were enjoying yourself, slut--"

"Alright," Kaliq moved so quickly that Kate and Jarrod were both caught off guard, "that's enough. Get out." He picked Jarrod up by his collar and grabbed his upper arm, shoving the smaller man toward the door. Jarrod struggled and stumbled along and there was nothing Kate could do but watch, slack jawed.

Kaliq shoved Jarrod out the door into the courtyard and yelled something in Arabic. Kate could read the language, but her spoken word skills left something to be desired and she couldn't quite make out what Kaliq had said. She guessed that he demanded that Jarrod be shown out.

She didn't know quite how to feel about the entire situation. She was angry and embarrassed by the way Jarrod had behaved, especially because he had called her a slut in front of Kaliq. She was grateful to Kaliq for rescuing her, but she also felt dumb for needing rescuing. She was shocked that Jarrod had actually had the nerve to paw at her like he had. She was dreading having to face Jarrod again at work, and she was even a teensy tiny bit worried that he really would be charged with some kind of crime.

"Thanks for saving me there," Kate blushed. "Dr. Cole's always been a jerk, but I never in a million years would have guessed that he was capable of anything that extreme. It never even occurred to me that he might actually be a dangerous person."

"You never know what direction danger is coming from," Kaliq swooped Kate into his arms and pressed his lips to hers.

Kate was so stunned that she froze and her eyes nearly popped from her head. She didn't push him away though. On the contrary, she practically melted into him. It wasn't any kind of intentional response; her body just reacted to Kaliq's in ways that were new to her.

Kaliq's tongue slipped past Kate's lips, searching for her own. She met his kiss with a hunger that came from deep inside of her belly. It burned through her veins and made her dizzy.

Fortunately for her, Kaliq was holding

her tightly in his arms. He was practically supporting all of her weight but Kate hadn't noticed how weak her knees had gone. The only thing she was aware of was his kiss.

He maneuvered her onto her back on one of the leather sofas in the dark room and positioned himself on top of her. Kate wrapped her legs around Kaliq's trunk and pulled him closer. She ran her hands through Kaliq's hair, which had come loose from it's restraint and was falling into his face and hers.

Kaliq broke their kiss and moved his lips to Kate's neck, where he lapped up the light layer of salt that had accumulated on her skin over the course of the hot night. He teased the sensitive area behind her ear and pressed himself into her sex, making her squirm in delight.

Kate wanted him. There was nothing she could do to conceal her desire. She had to have him, and judging by the way things were progressing, she was going to get what she wanted. Kaliq's kisses kept slipping lower and lower, from her neck down to her collarbone, then to the soft swell of her breasts.

Kate's eyelids fluttered open and she gazed at the high, dark ceiling. She could still hear the faint sounds of music and chatter wafting in from the courtyard. She knew that, at any moment, someone could walk in to find out what had happened between Kaliq and Jarrod.

She didn't care. She just needed Kaliq to keep doing what he was doing, which was moving further and further down her body. Kate briefly wondered whether she ought to sit up so that she could unzip the back of her dress. She began to stir, but Kaliq pushed her back down.

Once she settled back onto the sofa, Kate could feel Kaliq's rough hands on her thighs. He squeezed her and nestled his face in her belly, inhaling her fresh, soapy scent. Kate bucked her hips and grasped the pillow behind her.

There was something primal about the way Kaliq was taking her, especially after his confrontation with Jarrod. He was grasping at the tender flesh of her thighs like he was claiming her as his own. Kate desperately wanted to be claimed.

"Kaliq..." she moaned, not quite sure what she wanted to say to him. She wanted him to keep going where she thought he was headed, certainly, but she also wanted to ask him what *he* wanted. She wanted to know how to please him, and more so, she wanted to know his intentions. Was he drunk, like she was? Was he under the spell of some adrenalin rush, fueled by the confrontation?

Either way, Kate was afraid. Afraid that she'd get addicted to him. Afraid that she'd fool herself into thinking they had a future. Afraid that she'd get her heart broken when Kaliq inevitably forgot all about her.

Kaliq harbored no such fears. He crouched between Kate's knees and shoved her skirt up to her waist, exposing her embarrassingly utilitarian cotton panties. Kate hadn't exactly planned on meeting the man of her dreams in Samarra, and she hadn't packed anything sexy. Actually, she didn't own anything sexy. She definitely would have bought something if she had known that Kaliq was in her future.

Fortunately for her, he didn't seem to notice her panties. In fact, he was planting the lightest kisses all over her soft mound. Kate knew that those panties were soaked through; she could smell her own juices dripping. Kaliq was pressing his lips against her and she wondered whether he could taste her yet.

She needed more. Kate buried her fingers in Kaliq's hair and pressed his head into her mound. The scent of her sex mingled with the scents of desert flowers and exotic spices that wafted in from the courtyard and Kate could hear Kaliq groaning softly.

"Katie, let me taste you," Kaliq moaned into Kate's sex. "You smell so good."

He didn't need to ask. Kate wanted nothing more than his tongue on her wet slit. "Do it," she commanded. His eyes glanced up at hers and he grinned.

"Yes, ma'am," he laughed softly, pulling the crotch of her panties to the side. He didn't even bother to slip them off of her. Almost as soon as Kate could feel her lips exposed to the night air, Kaliq's tongue was on her. He drew it slowly along her labia, teasing her by taking his sweet time.

Kate bucked under him and he pushed her back down on the sofa. His tongue delved deep into her sex, curling and licking at her core. Kate moaned gently and wriggled beneath Kaliq's touch. He had his large palm on her belly and she took one of her hands out of his hair to intertwine her fingers with his.

After torturing her for what seemed like hours but was probably in actuality minutes, Kaliq finally slid his tongue over her most sensitive pearl. Kate thrust her hips and Kaliq slipped a hand under her butt, pulling her close.

Kaliq's other hand left Kate's belly and made its way to her soft folds. Kate could feel Kaliq's finger gently stroking her lips and she sucked in her breath. Then it happened. One of his big, strong fingers slipped past her labia into her aching pussy. Kate felt her body clench around it and she gyrated her hips in an attempt to feel more of him inside of her.

Kaliq began to gently fuck Kate with his middle finger as his tongue lashed her clit. God, he was like no man she'd ever been with. He was much, much bigger, for starters. He also seemed to know exactly what to do with his fingers and tongue to drive her wild. His finger curled up toward her belly and he stroked her in a way that she'd never felt before.

Kate briefly worried that Kaliq's skills were proof that he'd been with a lot of women. What he was doing felt so good, though, for the moment she didn't even care. She needed him to release that pressure that she could feel building in her body. Heat raced through her veins and her lower back tensed up. When that release she sought came, Kate had to bite her own shoulder to keep from screaming out. She was still at a party, after all, and she certainly didn't need to attract any attention.

Her body bucked and trembled with her orgasm as Kaliq continued his work. She could feel herself contracting around his finger and she desperately wanted his cock inside of her. Kate's eyes rolled back into her head and she rode the waves of her pleasure as they ripped through her until they died down.

She collapsed onto her back and felt Kaliq's finger slide out of her.

"That was incredible," she whispered to him.

"You're incredible," he answered, kissing her lips gently. "So sexy. You don't know how bad I want you right now."

"Take me," Kate was actually pretty spent, but she had a feeling that she could be back in the game in a few minutes if Kaliq touched her the right way.

"Not here, Katie. I'm afraid someone will walk in on us. Your friends are probably worried about you, especially if Dr. Cole made a scene when we threw him out. You're the sexiest woman I've ever met, but exhibitionism isn't really my thing." Kaliq smiled and held Kate close. "Besides, I've been too forward. I wouldn't want Dr. Cole to think I was a slut."

10

The following days were filled with work on the tunnels behind the lamassu. Jarrod had thankfully decided to pretend as though nothing out of the ordinary had taken place and that was perfectly fine with Kate. If he had assaulted her back home, she would have filed a complaint with the university overseeing their work. She wasn't interested in pursuing any sort of legal action in Samarra, however reprehensibly Jarrod had behaved. She was actually a little afraid about what Kaliq had said about the local repercussions.

At any rate, Kate was far more interested in her job than she was in punishing Jarrod Cole. The engineers on the team were hard at work, making sure that the tunnels were structurally sound. They crafted support beams and drew maps and even set up a generator and electric lights that illuminated the dark passageways.

Kate absolutely delighted in exploring the tunnels. Her big hope was to find a treasure trove of ancient artifacts, though she knew it wasn't likely. Locals had known about the tunnels for hundreds of years, so anything of value was probably long gone.

Still, it was exciting to explore the dark and winding passages carved into the mountain. Kate hadn't found any priceless antiquities, but she had spotted several small lizards and even a bat fluttering around. The more tunnel the engineers cleared, the deeper the caverns went.

Kate had already found the route up to the lookout, and she had also found a passage that led to a small room that was empty save for a few pottery shards. She wanted to go much deeper into the caves, but the engineers had forbidden it. They were afraid that the tunnels might collapse and she could be trapped or buried in debris.

Exploring the tunnels wasn't just fun; it was relevant to her work. Most scholars of ancient Samarri culture believed that the tunnels were used as a sort of backstage for political and religious ceremonies. Priests and rulers would use the area to prepare for public spectacles. Security would have been stationed throughout the passageways and lookouts.

Kate wasn't quite so sure. She had long suspected that the passages behind some of Samarra's giant sculpture were also used as housing, possibly for novice priests. She just needed to find out whether those tunnels led to any rooms, and looking for those rooms just happened to make her feel like Indiana Jones.

"Hey!" Mike jogged up to Kate, wearing a headlamp. "Simon says we can't go any further. They haven't cleared this tunnel yet."

Kate waited for him to catch up. "I was just gonna take a little peak. I just wanted to see what was up around that bend." That wasn't true. Kate had intended on doing a little secret exploring. Simon was the lead engineer on the team and he did great work, but he did it at a snail's pace. Kate suspected that he wouldn't clear the tunnel until he was absolutely certain that not a single pebble was loose.

Mike craned his neck around and peered into the darkness. "I don't know, Kate. Don't you think we should wait until the engineers do their thing?"

If Kate waited for the engineers, there was a chance that her funding would run out before she got through these tunnels. Hell, there was a chance that she would die of old age, at the rate things were going. She wasn't about to have this argument with Mike though.

"Yeah, you're probably right." Kate would just have to pretend to agree until he left. Mike was a research assistant and she was technically his boss, but exploring without the engineer's go-ahead was against the rules. Kate knew that Mike meant well, and she didn't want to get him into any kind of trouble or even put him in an uncomfortable position, but she just couldn't sit around and wait when there was so much exploring to be done.

"I should probably try to get better photographs from the lookout anyways. None of the shots I have really capture the detail in Fred's hair." God, that sounded dumb. It was true, though, both lamassu had long ringlets that were carved in intricate detail and Kate's picture taking skills weren't quite up to snuff.

"You want help?"

Jeez, take a hint, kid, Kate thought to herself. "Nah. Actually," she added, "do you think you could do me a favor and catalogue the pottery shards we found last week?" That little project would take him at least the entire afternoon.

"Sure! Do you want me to box them up too?"

That was the great thing about research assistants. Even the most mundane tasks were new and exciting. Kate gave Mike a list of things that he could take care of and he jogged off through the tunnels back to the tents, eager to get started.

With Mike out of her hair, Kate was free to go on her little expedition. She waited until she was good and sure he was gone, then hiked the backpack she'd packed with things like an extra headlamp, a flashlight, a notebook, pencils to sketch, and other random stuff up onto her shoulders. She gave a whistle so Banjo would follow her and set off down the dark trail.

Simon and his crew had cordoned off the unsecured area with several strands of yellow tape that read "Do Not Cross." Kate didn't want anyone to know that she was transgressing the engineering department's boundaries, so instead of tearing the ribbon down, she did a sort of crawl through like she was Spiderwoman. Banjo just trotted right underneath.

Kate knew that she had to hurry down the first part of the passage because she didn't want anyone to see her on the wrong side of the "Do Not Cross" tape. She and her dog scampered down the twenty meters or so that were still slightly illuminated by the tunnel's electric lighting system.

Then they reached the bend that Kate had been so eager to follow. She took one last quick look behind her, flicked on her headlamp, and pressed forward. Adrenalin surged through Kate's veins. She just felt like she was on top of the world. Her work was exciting and important, and the most gorgeous guy she'd ever laid eyes on seemed like he might really be into her.

It was funny the way a little attention from the right guy could make you feel like a whole new woman. Kate had always considered herself to be a pretty major dork. She had certainly been treated that way by the opposite sex until recently.

She was a hopeless case when it came to following trends. She'd made a number of misguided efforts over the years, including flat ironing her hair until it was literally breaking off, trying to cover her freckles with so much makeup that she looked like an amateur geisha, and wasting her parents' money on fashion blunders like rhinestone-studded designer jeans in an effort to fit in with the cool kids.

Kate still cringed when she thought of those jeans. She'd begged and begged her mother for them, they cost over a hundred bucks, and then they hadn't even fit her properly. They were made for tall, willowy girls. Not girls with little-boy bodies. She had worn them though, religiously, until the rhinestones fell off the back pockets.

All that seemed like ancient history now though. Pre-history, even. Kate felt like an entirely different woman. She felt mysterious, powerful, and sexy. She felt like the kind of woman who explored long-abandoned subterranean tunnels in faraway lands alone except for her spunky dog.

Poor Banjo wasn't so certain of himself. Kate was making her way slowly but confidently down the dark tunnel, careful to keep an eye out for any sign of danger, but moving rather sure-footedly considering the circumstances. She hadn't had to travel around the bend for long before the tunnel was pitch-black. Apparently, poor Banjo was afraid of the dark. He kept so close to Kate's feet that she was more in danger of tripping over him than over a rock. He was also whimpering softly, but he didn't abandon her, loyal friend that he was.

Kate regretted bringing him, for his own sake. He was clearly frightened, and it's not like he could have saved her from any potential disaster anyways. He'd probably do a great job scaring rats off with his bark, but Kate could tell that he'd rather be snoozing on her cot.

She wondered what Kaliq would think if he could see her. Would he be impressed? He seemed to like the fact that she was obsessed with her work. He encouraged her to talk about it in detail and he even asked questions. Maybe he would have liked to join her on this adventure. God, that would have been hot. The two of them, discovering the relics of lost civilizations, facing untold dangers in caves that no man (or woman) had entered for hundreds of years.

Kate's imagination was running away from her because the dark tunnel she was exploring seemed to have no end. She and Banjo progressed further and further into the mountain without encountering a single chamber or even a turn. Whatever this particular tunnel let to was buried deep, deep within the mountain.

Kate hoped that it was something important. She hoped that it was proof that the tunnels were used as housing, or she hoped that at least she'd find some really cool pottery or something like an ancient storage closet still filled with supplies for whatever ceremonies might be held at the lamassu.

The longer she walked, though, the less certain she was that she really ought to be in that tunnel alone. She desperately wanted to discover what was at the other end herself, but it was so dark. Kate was beginning to get the feeling that maybe Simon was right and she shouldn't be alone so deep in the mountain before his team had confirmed that the tunnels weren't on the brink of collapse.

She hated to do it, but Kate turned back for camp. She'd have to explore the tunnels another day. She could barely see around her with the little light that her headlamp gave off anyways, and if she got hurt, the entire project might lose funding. It just wasn't responsible for her to press on despite the potential danger.

At least Banjo was thrilled with her decision. The speed and alacrity with which the little dog bound back to camp made Kate suspect that he could actually see in the dark much better than she could. In fact, she could barely keep up with him.

The journey back out seemed to take only a fraction of the time the journey in had required. Kate and Banjo had made it about a hundred meters in, and as far as she could tell when she emerged back in the light, no one had noticed her short absence.

She dusted off her khakis and headed up to the lookout. She might as well get those pictures that she had mentioned to Mike, since the light was still good. She'd be able to revisit that tunnel soon enough. Besides, who knew. Maybe next time she went in, instead of Banjo, she'd have Kaliq at her side.

11

"You can't be serious."

Kate heard Jarrod's voice before she saw him, and instead of scampering off before he spotted her like she usually did, she hung around. Something about his tone told her that she needed to hear what he was worried over.

"That's impossible!"

She couldn't hear the person he was addressing. He might have been on the phone. Kate crept up as close to the meeting tent as possible and tried to determine exactly where Cole was sitting so that she could sidle up as near as possible without being detected.

"I need to speak to the Sheikha al Abbas immediately." Jarrod paused for just a second. "I demand to speak to the Sheikha!"

Kate ran into the tent. She didn't know what was going on, but she knew that Jarrod was having some kind of conniption fit and he probably didn't need to address the Sheikha in the state he was in.

"What is it?" Kate mouthed to Jarrod, her face riddled with concern.

"They're trying to shut us down," he practically cried to her. "They want us to halt the dig immediately."

"What?" Kate gasped back. "What?" Just like that, the rug had been pulled out from under her. In a single moment, Kate went from feeling like she had won at life, with the perfect job and the perfect boyfriend, to feeling like she was a complete failure whose dreams had just slipped right through her fingers.

Was it her fault? God, if this disaster had anything to do with her dealings with Kaliq, she'd never forgive herself. She'd deserve any abuse that Jarrod heaped upon her, for behaving unprofessionally and being selfish. For thinking that her pride was worth sacrificing the entire dig.

"Well, then, when is she available?" Jarrod continued his phone conversation. "Yes, that's fine. We can meet immediately. Yes, of course. Thank you." He hung up the phone, closed his eyes, and ran his fingers through his hair. He took a deep breath, then addressed Kate. "It's fucking al Hamar."

Kate was dumbfounded. "What?" She hadn't expected to hear that name. On the one hand, she was relieved that this setback had nothing to do with her. On the other, an issue with General al Hamar seemed quite a bit more serious than an issue with her crush.

"Fucking al Hamar. That asshole held a press conference this morning. He claimed that Samarra's border claims were illegal. He says Sanaar's border extends two hundred kilometers past the border established by Samarra and the lamassu are on his side."

Kate rolled her eyes and groaned. She'd known, in theory, that General al Hamar could cause problems for the dig. The General had recently led a coup against Sanaar's last dictator, and no one in the international community was surprised when al Hamar progressed almost instantaneously from being a devout communist to being another dictator.

He'd been rattling his saber for the past several weeks, making absurd threats against Samarra and a few other bordering countries. No one had actually believed that he would make any kind of move though. He was barely clinging to power in his own country and didn't really have the resources to invade his neighbors.

Kate bit her bottom lip. The General was

known for making empty threats. Why did his latest mean that the dig had to come to a halt?

"Did he specifically mention the lamassu?" she asked Jarrod.

Her colleague nodded. "It gets worse," he was almost on the brink of tears. "He said that the lamassu are religious icons that were used to poison the people's minds and they shouldn't be worshipped."

"That's ridiculous," Kate interjected. "No one has actually worshipped them for hundreds of years. They're historical artifacts."

"He's going to destroy them."

"What?!?"

"He claimed that he's going to free the people from religious oppression by destroying them."

"What the fuck?" Kate couldn't help but to exclaim. "That's the stupidest thing I've ever heard."

"I know. It seems as though al Hamar is willing to do anything to grab the attention of the international media. Still. The Sheikha's secretary called to halt the dig."

"Surely Samarra isn't going to just *let* al Hamar destroy their cultural artifacts."

"No, but the Sheikha can no longer guarantee our safety at the site. She wants us to clear out until the situation is settled."

"I think we should stay." Kate had no idea what had just come out of her mouth. That was the stupidest idea ever. Not only was it probably at least somewhat dangerous, if al Hamar really did try to make good on his threat, someone could get hurt -- it would probably also result in the Sheikha withdrawing her support unequivocally.

"Really?" Jarrod looked surprised. "Well I can't say that I want to pack up and leave either. I don't see how we could just blatantly disregard the Sheikha's request, though, since she's the one paying for all this."

"Did I hear right that she's granted us a meeting?"

"She did. She's coming tomorrow afternoon."

"Okay," Kate paced back and forth through the tent, trying to formulate a plan of action. "Here's what we're going to do. We'll give everyone the rest of the afternoon off, so we're technically not disobeying the Sheikha's directive. Then you and I can brainstorm and come up with an argument that will convince her to let us keep working until al Hamar shows his true colors and a threat is imminent." Kate paused here to look at Jarrod. "That's reasonable. The Sheikha knows as well as we do that the General usually doesn't follow through on these threats."

Jarrod nodded. "It could work. Her assistant made it sound like there was no room for negotiation, but maybe the Sheikha can be reasoned with."

"We need to see that press conference."

Jarrod pulled up his laptop. The internet at the site could be a bit spotty, but it wasn't abysmal. He powered up and typed "hamar press conference" into his search engine.

Up came a series of results that had nothing to do with the lamassu. Apparently, al

Hamar had been giving a press conference about something or other nearly every day for the past several weeks. There were press conferences about local politics, international politics, aid programs, structural changes in the military, education initiatives, and Sanaari prisons.

Jarrod kept scrolling and they found recent press conferences about criminal charges for opposition members, the nationalization of a few businesses that belonged to supporters of the last dictator, and the destruction of Sanaar's public libraries. Things seemed pretty rough in that neighboring country. The General was cracking down hard on any and all opposition, plus he was pulling stunts like destroying local monuments and firing entire faculties from Sanaar's universities so that he could fill their positions with his own lackeys.

So far, though, there was no evidence that al Hamar had actually made good on any of his threats to neighboring countries. There was just a lot of blustering and wild claims. Hamar seemed to especially have it in for the al Abbas family. There were a great many videos of him accusing them and their associates of everything from election fraud to arms dealing. There was even one of him accusing them of somehow causing Sanaar's stray dog problem.

"This dude is nuts," Kate observed aloud as Jarrod continued to scroll. "You think he's really crazy, or you think this is some kind of strategy?"

"I don't know," Jarrod answered. "Why the hell can't I find today's press conference."

"Try 'Hamar border dispute Samarra' or something like that?"

Jarrod responded by typing in 'hamar lamassu destruction,' probably just to irritate Kate. Even when they had a mutual goal, he couldn't resist the urge to be as contrary as possible. Kate had to suppress a smile when nothing came up. This wasn't the time for petty grievances.

Next he tried 'Sanaar samarra conflict.' This time Kate just had to roll her eyes. Of course that wasn't going to work; half of the videos were about various aspects of the conflict. Finally he gave up and typed in 'hamar border dispute samarra.' *Bam*, there it was, first result.

On any other day, Kate probably would have made some smart ass comment to Jarrod. At this particular moment, however, she knew better than to provoke him into bickering with her. She needed his cooperation and she didn't have the patience to deal with any more of his childishness than was necessary.

Jarrod clicked play. The video buffered and the now-familiar face of General al-Hamar appeared on the screen. Even though he'd seized power months ago, he still wore his military uniform at all times. He was a big, burly man with a big, brushy mustache. He kind of reminded Kate of a Sanaari version of Colonel Mustard.

He was at a long table in front of some gold drapery. Kate didn't recognize the location, but she guessed that it was either the former prime minister's palace or possibly a luxury hotel's conference room. There were at least a dozen microphones in front of him, and Kate could make out the reflection of camera flashes on the General's oily skin.

"Thank you for joining me here today for this groundbreaking historical event."

Kate audibly groaned. Groundbreaking historical event? By the looks of things, Hamar had given more meaningless political speeches in the past six months than many world leaders gave in their entire lives.

"For too long, the people of Sanaar have been living under oppression."

This was true. The ordinary citizens of Sanaar had it rough. The country seemed to be in a constant state of upheaval, and of course that meant that things like health and education suffered.

"Our people have lived under the yoke of dictatorship."

His people continued to live under the yoke of dictatorship, but Kate suspected that wasn't going to be a part of Hamar's speech.

"They've lived under the constant threat of foreign invasion."

This was only true insofar as the United Nations had repeatedly threatened to send peacekeeping troops.

"And in one of the most recent and audacious examples of foreign aggression against the culture, tradition, and very existence of Sanaar, the United States' puppet government in Samarra has attempted to steal our land by redrawing our borders."

Accusing other governments of being manipulated by either the West, Russia, or China was one of Hamar's favorite tactics. Depending upon his mood on any particular day, you could find him accusing pretty much any of the world's superpowers of the most ridiculous, insignificant, completely imaginary schemes that you could dream up.

"The attack on the Sanaari people isn't just physical," the General continued, "but ideological. The Samarri made a deal with the United States to steal Sanaari land because they wanted to take ownership of the giant religious idols that have poisoned the mind of working people for hundreds of years. I'm here today to tell you that Sanaar will not take this attack on our land and our culture laying down! Effective immediately, I am restoring the traditional borders of Sanaar, two hundred kilometers to the west of the fraudulent border drawn by the Samarri pretenders."

Kate could hear some kind of commotion happening in front of the General, but couldn't make out what it was. The General paused until the room was silent once more and the camera flashes died down.

"Furthermore," he continued, "the Sanaari people have lived under the shadow of religious delusion for too long." Here he paused for dramatic effect once more. "The idols are coming down!"

At this point, the screen lit up with camera flashes. The General only allowed his lackeys to photograph and interview him, so the "journalists" present at the press conference asked him a series of questions like "when did the inspiration to free the Sanaari people from religious oppression come to him?" and "what steps are being taken to protect the Sanaari people from further Samarri aggression?"

Jarrod hit pause on the video. "Well," he stated, staring off into space. "That was really something."

"He sounded serious," Kate agreed. "Do you think he's bluffing? What would he even use to take them down? Bulldozers?"

"I don't know," Jarrod shook his head. "But it looks like we have our work cut out for us.

12

Kate's second official meeting with
Ghazal al Abbas had her flustered. She was
willing to do anything to protect her work on the
lamassu, up to and including risking her own
safety. Not that she actually believed that General
al Hamar would invade Samarra and destroy a
pair of ancient, giant artifacts that didn't even

belong to him.

The biggest risk that Kate perceived was actually the Sheikha herself. Kate could understand the Sheikha's point of view; she obviously didn't want a project that she sponsored to end violently. Of course she wanted to be as conservative as possible when it came to the safety of the people who worked on her project.

Kate didn't truly believe that anyone's safety was at stake, though, and she suspected that the Sheikha wasn't entirely convinced by the General's threats either. Plus, if the Sheikha pulled the plug on the dig, the team could only wait around in Samarra for so long before they ran out of time and money and had to return to their regular positions at universities across America.

Thus it was that Kate sat down at the desk in her room and tugged at the ends of her hair. She had to come up with something good, something convincing and reassuring.

"So we need to make the Sheikha

understand that she's going to be the big loser if she shuts the dig down," Jarrod strode into Kate's tent, even though they'd already agreed that he would handle telling the crew they had the day off. He'd apparently decided that his time was better spent annoying Kate. "We have to show her that she can't just interrupt our work on a whim."

Kate sat up and glared at Jarrod. "Jarrod, she's holding all the cards here. She can cut off our resources with the snap of a finger. Hell, she could probably have us deported, if that's what she wanted. I really think that in this case, we'll catch more flies with honey than vinegar, if you know what I mean."

"So you think we should appeal to her emotions?"

Kate had enough experience working with Jarrod to know that the best way to get him off her back was to flatter him. She hated to do it. She was particularly worried about giving him the wrong idea, namely the idea that she liked or admired him, especially considering his recent stunt. She just didn't have the time to deal with his crap at the moment.

"Yes. I'll appeal to her emotions. Your cold logic would probably just fluster her." Kate wondered if she'd laid it on too thick. She hadn't meant to sound so sarcastic, but she couldn't help it.

"You're probably right," Jarrod nodded.

Kate breathed a sigh of relief. He was so vain that it hadn't occurred to him that she was not being completely sincere. "We wouldn't want her to get upset."

"Yeah, who knows how she'd react. She is pretty impulsive. Okay, here's what we'll do. You put together something that will tear at her heartstrings or whatever you think it is that will appeal to her, and I'll give the orders to shut everything down."

"Great. I'll get right on it." That was exactly what they'd already agreed to do twenty minutes prior, but evidently Jarrod needed to feel like he was in charge before he could complete even the most basic task.

At least he finally left her alone. Kate

had about an hour to prepare for the meeting. By the time she heard the Sheikha's entourage pulling up, she felt as ready as she was ever going to be. She quickly threw on a clean shirt, smoothed out her hair, and went to greet Ghazal.

"Kate, sweetheart, come here." The Sheikha surprised Kate by embracing her. "I'm so sorry." Ghazal frowned and pat her on the back.

"Thanks, Sheikha."

"Ghazal, please dear."

"Ghazal. Did you want to talk in the tent? It's a bit more comfortable than out here in the sun."

"Yes, of course. Kaliq!" Ghazal called behind her.

Kate was surprised. She hadn't expected to see Kaliq that afternoon. Crap. Now she was not only worried about impressing the Sheikha, she was also worried about not looking like a pathetic dork in front of the man of her dreams.

Kaliq stepped out of his step-mother's Land Rover. He looked like he had just stepped from the pages of GQ. He was wearing a gorgeous tailored suit and his shoulder-length hair was pulled back in a slick ponytail. Kate wondered whether this meeting had interrupted some other important al Abbas family business.

"Kate," Kaliq kissed her on the cheek. Kate wasn't sure whether Ghazal was aware of their relationship, or whether it would help or hinder her cause today.

The group made their way to the conference tent. It was just the four of them, Kate, Kaliq, Jarrod, and Ghazal. Kate and Jarrod had decided not to tell the rest of the team about Hamar's threat until they knew for sure whether or not they'd be shut down. They didn't want to start a panic or damage the team's morale.

The many empty seats at the table made the meeting feel much more casual than the first one, though the stakes were considerably higher. Kate felt more like she was having an informal get together in the lunch room than a serious meeting to determine the future of her work.

They got seated and Kate caught Kaliq glaring at Jarrod. Jarrod wouldn't even meet the

Sheikh's eyes.

"Thank you so much for agreeing to meet us here today," Kate began, hoping that neither Jarrod nor Kaliq would cause any kind of distraction. "We wanted to talk to you about Hamar's threat."

"Yes," Ghazal nodded. "Terrible. I'm so sorry that you have to deal with this madman. He's been causing us headaches for months. I don't want you to feel unsafe, though. I can promise you that your safety is our number one priority here." The Sheikha laid a hand over Kate's. She really had a way about her that made Kate feel like she cared.

"Thank you so much for your help, Ghazal. I've discussed the threat with Jarrod, and we'd actually like to ask your permission to keep working unless Hamar actually makes a move. We've been following his threats and it seems clear to us that he's bluffing. He doesn't have the resources to invade, and I suspect that he doesn't actually have any desire either."

Ghazal pursed her lips. "Darling, I don't

think he'd dare either. But we simply can't take risks like that. Can you imagine what I'd have to tell your poor mother if something happened to you on this project? Did you know that this man put my daughter-in-law in a men's prison once?"

Kate's eyebrows went up. No, she certainly hadn't known that. She'd only met Michelle al Abbas for a minute, but nothing about the woman had screamed "adventuress" to her.

"Sheikha al Abbas," Jarrod interrupted, "if you're worried about Dr. Delaney's safety, we could replace her with a man. I could take over her responsibilities and hire an assistant for myself."

All three pairs of eyes turned to Jarrod. Kate wanted to murder him, again.

"I can assure you," Ghazal replied with ice in her voice, "that your parents would be just as grieved as Kate's if something were to happen to you. Do I need to remind you that I only have sons?"

"Certainly not," Jarrod flushed, "I just thought--"

"I can provide security," Kaliq interjected. Everyone at the table turned from Jarrod to him. "I can bring my own security detail and we can patrol the dig so that Dr. Delaney can continue working safely. It's no trouble at all. I already have the manpower and I'm eager to see these tunnels excavated."

He sounded so sincere that for a moment, Kate believed that he was so interested in archaeology that he couldn't bear to see the dig slowed down.

The lady Ghazal had one eyebrow raised. "Are you sure, Kaliq? You'd know that this conflict could last for several months."

"Of course. I can get started tomorrow, I just need to notify my staff. There's no reason why we should let this dog Hamar intimidate us."

Ghazal considered his proposition. "Well, I must say, I can't really take this threat seriously. Is this what you want?"

Kate waited for Kaliq to respond before realizing that the question had been addressed to her. "Me?" she stuttered, caught off guard. "Yes.

Thank you so much, Sheikh al Abbas, yes. That's such a generous offer."

Kate didn't hear much of the conversation that followed between the al Abbas family and Jarrod. She was stunned. Had Kaliq really just offered to stand guard? Kate shook her head. No, that was ridiculous. That wasn't what he'd said. He'd said that he was going to *provide* security, not that he was going to *be* security. He was going to loan the dig his private security force.

Well, that wasn't quite as exciting as having her own personal hunk bodyguard, but it was very generous and it did save the day. The dig was still on, and now they'd have extra security. They probably didn't need it, but it couldn't hurt.

Plus, Kate hoped, maybe Kaliq would come around more to check up on things. Ever since their last night of passion, he'd made himself scarce. Kate knew that he was very busy, though she had no idea exactly what it was that he'd done, but she was beginning to feel a bit like she was getting blown off again.

It would be nice it she could figure out where she stood with him. It was even nicer that her work would continue uninterrupted. Kate and Jarrod walked the Sheikha back to her ride and thanked her again for her time and support.

"Auntie, I need to speak to Kate about a few details. Go ahead and I'll keep one of the other cars here to ride back." Kaliq kissed Ghazal on the cheek and she left, followed by most of her entourage.

Kate had wondered about Kaliq's relationship with his father's wives. She'd imagined that they were like stepmothers, and Ghazal had referred to Kaliq as her son, but he'd just addressed her as Auntie.

"Dr. Cole, please leave us," Kaliq wasn't so warm with Jarrod. The smaller man scampered off and left the couple alone to chat.

"Kaliq, you didn't need to do this," Kate assured him, a little worried that he felt obligated.

He surprised her by grasping her face in his strong hands, right there in public where anyone could see. "Kate, look at me. I made a mistake when I didn't reveal my identity the day we met. I've given you the wrong impression, and you have every reason to believe I'm not a sincere or honest man."

Kate tried to shake her head "no" but he was holding her too tightly so she let him continue.

"I'm going to make it up to you. I'm going to show you what kind of man I am. I promise that no one will hurt you while you are in my country. Give me the opportunity to prove to you that I'm worthy of your trust. You won't be disappointed."

Kate felt the color flush to her cheeks. She'd never been the recipient of a grand romantic gesture. "This is the nicest thing anyone has ever done for me," she finally answered.

Kaliq planted a firm but chaste kiss right on her lips. "Just give me another chance."

Kate was perfectly willing to give him another chance without the armed guard, but it certainly didn't hurt. She stood and watched his

Land Rover recede into the distance.

"Well," a familiarly grating voice started, too close to her ear, "that was unexpected."

"Yeah," Kate had to agree.

"Who would have guessed that your efforts to sleep your way to the top would benefit us all."

"Jarrod," Kate finally turned, looking directly into his smug face.

"Yeah?"

"Shut the fuck up."

13

The next morning was business as usual, all thanks to Kaliq's promise. Kate rolled out of bed, threw on a pair of mostly-clean pants and a tank top, whistled for Banjo, and headed out to grab some breakfast.

As soon as she stepped out of her tent, it

was immediately evident that things were different. Kate spotted a veritable armada of shiny black SUVs parked at the edge of the camp. There were men yelling in Arabic, though she couldn't see anyone yet, and none of the camp's regular workers were anywhere to be seen.

She made her way to the dining tent and ran smack into Kaliq.

"Careful!" he laughed, grasping her shoulders.

"Hey!" Kate smiled, happy to see him. "Oh my God, is that a gun?" He was wearing some kind of big gun on his back. Kate wasn't a firearms aficionado, but she was pretty sure that she was looking at an automatic rifle. "Jesus Christ, Kaliq, I'm sure that's not necessary."

"Sweetheart, this isn't Minnesota."

"It isn't Kabul either," Kate stepped back from Kaliq's embrace.

"Look, Katie, we both hope that this threat will blow over into nothing. In all likelihood, that's what will happen. But if you want to keep working here, we need to be safe.

You don't know al Hamar like I do. This is not a nice man. Not even a reasonable man. He doesn't have any respect for other people at all, especially not friends of my family and especially not women. If you want to keep working here, you need to let me keep my promise."

"I just really don't think a big gun like that is necessary. Maybe a pistol?" That seemed like a good compromise.

"Katie, you're going to have to give up control if you want my protection." Kaliq stepped forward and stroked Kate's cheek. Kate didn't like the prospect of working around so many heavily armed men, but it was looking like she didn't have a choice. "My men are trained experts. You don't have anything to worry about. Do you trust me?"

Kate looked up into Kaliq's jade eyes. She wanted to give up and put her faith in him, but her nagging subconscious just wouldn't let her.

She didn't know if it was him she couldn't trust, or herself. She was still finding it impossible to truly believe that a man like Kaliq would care about a woman like her. He seemed genuine, but his initial deception and her obvious inadequacies kept sending shivers of apprehension through her which made her second-guess everything he did or said.

Still, it wasn't like her insecurities were even relevant to the issue of whether or not he took gun safety seriously. She couldn't even explain to him why the prospect of trying to do her archaeological work surrounded by soldiers unsettled her.

"I guess I don't have a choice," she answered, looking off at the lamassu in the distance.

Kaliq kissed the top of her head. "I guess not," he replied. "Anyways, this isn't a social call. Get back to work, Dr. Delaney," he joked, smacking her on the butt.

"Kaliq!" Kate's eyes went wide.

"Sorry," he grinned. "That was unprofessional. Hardly appropriate for a hired gun."

"Well, to be fair, I think it would be more

accurate to say that I work for you," Kate finally cracked a smile.

"Actually we both work for my Auntie. We'd better quit fooling around before we get caught." Kaliq blew Kate one last kiss and marched off toward whatever it is he had to do.

Kate stood and watched Kaliq from behind. He was wearing combat boots, a black T shirt, and black pants with cargo pockets. He looked like some kind of special forces guy, not a sensitive artist.

He really was something of a chameleon, always changing his skin. One moment he was a romantic painter, the next moment a sleek businessman, and the next a soldier. Kate almost felt like she didn't know him at all.

Yet there was something about Kaliq that drew her in, and it wasn't just his money and looks. Kaliq made Kate feel like the world was full of great opportunities. Not only that, but he made her feel like maybe she could accomplish great things. He was just so sure of himself that she guessed that his attitude must have rubbed off on her a little bit.

Confidence wasn't going to get her very far if all she did was stand around and moon over boys, though, so Kate proceeded to breakfast. Once she got to the tent, she ran right into Mike.

"Dude," he started, looking very unsettled, "what's with all the Rambos? Is something bad happening?"

"Eh," Kate wanted to be honest. "You know who General al Hamar is?" she waited for Mike to answer but he just tilted his head to the side. "He's the guy that just took over the country next door," she explained. "He's not really a big deal on the international scene but he's pretty famous for making outrageous claims about other countries."

"Like what kind of stuff?"

"Like saying that the United States conducted a secret operation to infect Sanaari children with tuberculosis."

"I hope that's not true," Mike looked alarmed.

"It is very unlikely. Anyhow, yesterday he

said that the lamassu actually belong to Sanaar and not Samarra and that the Samarri people have no right to conduct this dig."

"Whoa," Mike nodded. "So what's with the soldiers? Are the Samarri peeps afraid that this Hamar dude will try to steal the lamassu?"

"He wants to destroy them, actually. So the al Abbas clan sent a guard to protect them."

"Shit. Are we in danger?"

It hadn't even occurred to Kate that she was putting her entire team at risk. She just hadn't taken the threat seriously at all. Her only thought had been protecting her work, but now that Mike seemed legitimately concerned for his safety, she felt guilty. "No. I mean, there's a slight chance that Hamar's troops actually do show up, but it's very doubtful. He's made a ton of threats lately and hasn't acted on any of them. Anyhow, the al Abbas sent this extra security, so we're fine. If Hamar does make a move, we'll evacuate and let the security deal with it."

"I saw your man is their boss. Didn't that guy tell you he was an artist?"

"Yeah, I guess he's also a part time commando," Kate joked. She had no idea how else to answer that question, so humor seemed like the best tack to take.

"Lifestyles of the rich and famous, I guess," Mike smiled. "Hey, you should lock that down. Then you can become an archeologist slash ninja slash lifestyle blogger or something."

Kate spent the rest of the morning in high spirits. Jarrod was nowhere to be seen, but she could spot Kaliq up high on the lookout next to the lamassu. He looked fantastic in his soldier get up, if Kate was being completely honest with herself. Even from her secret spot in one of the tents she sometimes used as an office, she could make out the bulging muscles underneath of his tight black T shirt.

Kate had worried that having Kaliq on the site would make her nervous and self-conscious. He'd avoided her the entire day, probably on purpose so that he didn't interrupt her work, so she hadn't felt like he was watching everything she did.

Instead, she pretty much wasted the day watching everything he did. She watched as he squatted down on his thick haunches and surveyed the site. She watched as he gave directions to the men he'd brought with him. She watched as he patrolled back and forth at the site's perimeters. Hardly half an hour passed between breaks she took to leer at him.

At least he couldn't see her gawking. Kate had a very discreet lookout spot of her own. She was in a tent with a net window, so she could see out but from far away it was difficult to see in. She pretended to work on organizing her notes, while taking every chance available to peek at her new security detail.

By the time dinner rolled around, she'd successfully filed approximately eight documents. Kate knew that she couldn't spend all day, every day staring at Kaliq. One slow afternoon wasn't really going to hurt though.

She'd kept him under such constant surveillance that he really took her by surprise when he snuck up on her in the mess hall. "Hey," his warm breath tickled her ear as she gave a jump. "How'd I do?"

Kate raised her eyebrows.

"I thought you'd be the best person to ask, since you didn't take your eyes off of me the entire day."

"That isn't true." It was true, and Kate was blushing.

Kaliq laughed. "Did you think I couldn't see you there in your little office? Anyhow, now you owe me."

"I owe you?"

"Yes. You owe me."

"For what?"

"For the show. I was here on guard duty capacity, not as eye candy. Now you have to pay me back."

"How?"

"You have to let me draw you."

"Okay, go ahead."

"I mean you have to model for me."

"What? Like one of your French girls? No way."

"My French girls?"

"It's from a movie."

"What happens in the movie?"

"The guy draws the girl naked."

"Whoa, I was just suggesting that you sit for me. If you want to take off your clothes, though," Kaliq slipped his arm around Kate's waist, "who am I to stop you?"

"What? I'm not going to let you draw me naked."

"Hey, it was your idea, doc. You American girls really are as brazen as they say."

"You're sneaky."

"So? What do you say? Will you sit for me? Clothes on, if you insist."

Kate had to consider the proposition. No one had ever drawn her portrait before. She wasn't sure she wanted to see herself the way Kaliq saw her. "Okay," she took the plunge, thinking that she'd just embarrass herself even more by revealing her crippling insecurities about her looks. "You're on. When are we doing this?"

"How about right now?"

"In the mess hall?"

"Is there somewhere more private we could go?"

"Follow me."

Kate led Kaliq out of the mess tent, through the camp's still-light alleys and around the tents they used as offices. They passed a number of her coworkers who greeted them but didn't seem to think there was anything weird at all about her showing the Sheikh through the camp. Kate wondered whether they assumed she was on official business or whether they cared less about her romantic intrigues than she had assumed.

At any rate, she was still a little nervous when she got to her own tent. She peeked around to make sure that no one was looking, then pulled the Sheikh inside.

"Will this work?" she asked, turning to face him.

Kaliq pulled Kate into his arms and thrust his tongue into her mouth. Kate was too surprised by his kiss to respond with anything more than a whimper. Fortunately, her body seemed to know exactly what to do. She melted into his tight embrace and welcomed his hungry kiss.

Kaliq had to bend his knees to grab Kate's pert ass, but once he got a good grip she could feel his fingers pressing into her soft flesh. He pulled her close and Kate could feel his cock stirring through their clothing.

"My God, I've wanted to do this all day," Kaliq groaned, breaking their kiss for just a moment so that he could turn his attention to her pale neck. His hot lips brushed the sensitive skin just behind her earlobe. "I want to taste every freckle on your body."

"Kaliq," Kate moaned back. "What are we doing?"

"We're doing exactly what you've been thinking about doing all day. I'm finally going to have you."

14

"Kaliq..."

"I wasn't sure you wanted this until I saw you watching me today." Kaliq lifted Kate by her butt so she could wrap her legs around his tree trunk of a waist. He took her bottom lip into his teeth and nibbled it gently. "I didn't want you to think you were under any obligation to me."

Obligation? Kate had no idea what the hell he was talking about. It didn't seem to matter though. All that mattered to her in that very moment was that he not stop. She buried her fingers in his thick, shiny hair and pushed her tongue past his lips, searching for his. She could taste the bitter tea that everyone in Samarra seemed to love, and that taste was at once both familiar and exotic.

Kate's fingers moved from Kaliq's hair to his solid shoulders, where she grasped his T shirt and pulled up, up, up until his well defined abs were exposed.

Kaliq laughed a low, throaty laugh and set Kate on her desk for a second while he peeled the shirt off. Kate's eyes traveled up and down his golden caramel skin, taking in every drop of him. He had a pelt of curly black hair on his chest, which was totally new to Kate. All the guys she'd dated previously had been pale and hairless. Kaliq's furry chest made her think of lumberjacks, or maybe even bears.

She slipped her fingers through it and

could feel the firm, warm skin of his pecs beneath her hands. Her fingers slid down, over the ripples of his belly, to the buckle of his pants. Kate pulled the leather strap through the silver buckle, unbuttoned his pants, and freed his already hardening member.

Kaliq was much thicker than anyone else Kate had ever seen in real life. She wrapped her fingers around his velvety shaft and couldn't even touch the tip of her thumb to the tip of her middle finger. Kate had small hands, but not that small.

"Do I get to undress you?" Kaliq smiled, letting Kate look him over.

"I guess it's only fair," Kate answered, not meeting his gaze. She wanted to feel his amazing body inside of her own, but she still wasn't too crazy about him getting a good look at her. She was covered head to toe in freckles and her breasts weren't really any more impressive bare then they were clothed.

She didn't stop him, though, when he set to work on the buttons on her shirt. He flicked them open, one by one, and slipped the shirt from her shoulders. Kate bit the bullet and pulled off the tank top she was wearing underneath, exposing the rosy nubs she'd been so shy about.

Kaliq took a long, slow look at her, making her wish that she'd worn a bra. She couldn't tell by the expression on his face whether he liked what he was seeing. He cupped one of her small breasts in his hand and brushed his thumb over her pert nipple, causing her to clench the muscles in her stomach.

"They're so pink," he muttered, more to himself than to her. He licked his lips and Kate leaned into his touch, taking his cock into her hand once agains and stroking him gently.

Kaliq slipped his fingers into the waistband of Kate's pants and pulled her closer. He made short work of her own fly and slid her khakis and her boring white underwear under her butt. Kate kicked off her boots and Kaliq had her pants all the way off. While he was slipping out of his own pants, she pulled off her socks and tossed them aside.

"Do you taste like strawberries?" Kaliq asked. "Because that's what you look like. Strawberries and cream."

He picked her up and transported her to her cot, where he laid her on her back. He raised her arms above her head and pinned her wrists to her pillow so that he had full access to her warm, soft body. He planted a trail of light kisses that led from her throat, down her clavicle, and to the pointed tips of her breasts, sending waves of electricity through her veins.

Kaliq sucked one of Kate's nipples into his mouth and teased the sensitive tip with his tongue, swirling it around and suckling until Kate's breast ached just a little bit. She arched her back and struggled a little bit against his restraint; she wanted to grab a handful of his hair and guide him further south, but he held her tight as he played with her breasts.

A soft moan escaped from Kate's lips when Kaliq finally started moving further down. She still shivered at the memory of the last time he'd performed oral sex on her. The man could do things with his tongue that made her lose her mind.

He wasn't willing to give her what she wanted just yet though. Kaliq let Kate's wrists go and down her hands went to his hair. When she started guiding him down, however, he said "behave unless you want me to tie you up."

Kate's eyes popped open. Maybe she did want him to tie her up. She'd never been tied up. It sounded more like a threat than a promise, though, so for the time being she let him do his thing.

It turned out that his thing was torturing her. He made her suffer by making her wait for what she wanted, and she wasn't by nature a patient woman. Kaliq teased Kate by brushing his lips over her jutting hips, which he had to hold down because she couldn't help but to buck them. He traced his kissed all over her lower belly and the scruff from his beard tickled her and gave her goosebumps.

Kate seriously hoped that Kaliq wasn't going to make her beg. She was willing to do anything at that point to get his mouth on her pussy. She was already dripping wet and burning up with desire for him.

She really, really hoped that this encounter would lead even further than the last one. They were finally alone and they finally seemed to be on the same page. She had been daydreaming about him all day long and now that Kate had seen Kaliq's cock, she just had to have it inside of her.

Finally he made his move. Kaliq buried his face in Kate's red curls and lapped up the nectar dripping from her pink lips. His touch made her want to scream, but the tent walls weren't exactly soundproof and she didn't need the entire camp listening in, so she was forced to bite her lip.

Kaliq's tongue slipped up and down Kate's folds, never quite making it to her tender, hard clit. She knew that he meant to tease her, but even having his kiss on her lips felt so good. If he kept it up for long enough, Kate might be able to come from that alone.

He didn't tease her forever though. Just when she was really heating up and starting to lose control, he sucked her throbbing pink pearl into his plush lips. He let her bury her hands in his hair as he worked her hot button, lashing it with his tongue and then suckling on it.

Kate didn't think she could take any more. Then he added a finger and she completely lost it. He barely got the chance to penetrate her before she was bucking wildly beneath him, trying to keep her whimpers down.

"Kaliq, oh my God," she cried, as quietly as humanly possible. "Fuck..."

She could feel him smile. He crooked the finger inside of her into a sort of 'come hither' gesture and rubbed the inside of her tight passage with the pad of his finger as she convulsed around him.

When Kate's orgasm died down, Kaliq flipped her knees up to her ears. He got up on his own knees and let her rest her legs on his broad shoulders. His cock was so hard that it bounced gently as he moved.

"Is this what you want?" he asked, sliding the soft, spongy head up and down Kate's wet sex so that it became slick with her juices.

"Yes," Kate gasped back, watching his manhood glide over her.

"You want me to fuck you?"

"Yes, Kaliq. Do it," she bucked her hips as his head slipped over her aching clit.

"Like this?" he asked, slipping the head and the first few inches in. Already Kate could feel how thick he was, and it was incredible.

"More," she moaned.

"More?" he repeated, sliding just a little further in.

"I want all of you," Kate cried out.

Kaliq obliged. He gasped as he slid his long, fat cock into her tight pussy. Kate felt herself stretch to accommodate him and it hurt, just a little tiny bit, but in a good way. She knew that she'd be sore the next morning but it would be the delicious kind of soreness that came after she had overindulged in something that she really wanted.

"You really are a stunning woman, Katie," Kaliq watched Kate as she trembled beneath him. He was fucking her slowly and enjoying the feeling of her small body squeezing him. Kate could see his eyes pass over her throat, her small breasts, and her wide hips. He seemed sincere, and the added boost of confidence made Kate feel incredibly sexy and wanted.

She didn't know this, but Kaliq was admiring the flush that had spread over her entire body. Her ordinarily white, porcelain skin was dotted with hundreds of thousands of tiny freckles. When she was aroused, it seemed, her freckles expanded and her entire zones of her body including her chest, her face, her pretty throat, and her belly turned bright pink. It was the most adorable thing Kaliq had ever seen in his entire life and he made a mental note that they'd probably never be able to enjoy a discreet quicky. The blush in her skin would be a dead giveaway.

He wasn't intending to be quick that night. They had the entire night alone, as far as they knew no one knew they were together, and he intended to enjoy her. His body was screaming for him to take her like an animal, fuck her hard, and come deep inside of her. He had to fight back his urge to be rough and fast because he wanted to watch her come with his dick inside of her.

Kate could tell that Kaliq was doing everything in his power to control himself. She could see beads of sweat forming on his forehead, and his own chest had a ruddy glow. She wiggled her hips, eager for him to pound her a little harder. She was still so wound up from her first orgasm and she knew that it wouldn't take much to send her over the edge again.

Kate's head rolled back on her shoulders as Kaliq panted and sped up his pace the tiniest big. Over and over, his thick cock pushed inside of her small, tight body. Kate could feel the pressure building up in her core again.

"Kate," Kaliq gasped, "touch yourself for me."

Kate's hand snaked down her belly and the pad of her middle finger found her hard little clit. She stroked it in circles and had to close her eyes. It was almost like she was blinded by the pleasure that shot through her body. She shook and trembled and finally Kaliq let loose. He pounded her hard and fast, grasping the tops of her thighs so that she didn't slip away from him.

Kaliq couldn't hold out any longer. Kate's throbbing pussy milked the cream from his manhood, and his release came with a low groan. Once his dick stopped twitching, he released her legs from his shoulders and collapsed on top of her. Both of them were covered with sweat, and the scent of their bodies filled the air of the small tent.

Kaliq kissed Kate on the lips before he caught his breath. "Was it okay for you?"

Kate looked surprised. Okay? She had thought that it was pretty obvious from her behavior that it was incredible. "It was awesome," she assured her Sheikh. They laid quietly in each others' arms, relaxing and listening to the sounds of the desert night.

"Well," Kaliq finally started.

Kate picked up her head, seriously hoping that he wasn't about to say that he had to leave.

"Are you ready?"

"Ready for what?"

"Ready for me to draw you like one of my French girls," he grinned.

15

"Okay," Kate surprised herself. Normally the thought of being scrutinized while naked would have horrified her, but in that particular moment she was feeling like a million bucks. "What do I do?"

Kaliq sat upright. "Okay, first I need

some paper and a pencil."

Kate leaned over and pulled a pencil and a notepad from the drawer on her nightstand. She flipped past several pages of notes until she came to a blank page. "Will this do?" she asked, handing Kaliq the pad.

"Perfect," he answered. "Now strike a pose that makes you comfortable."

"Like this?" Kate asked with one hand behind her head and one on her hip.

Kaliq scrunched up his face. "Try something more natural," he adjusted her arms so that they were both behind her head, "maybe like this."

Kate had to admit, the position was much more comfortable. She bent one knee and turned her head to the side so that she had a better view of Kaliq.

"That's perfect," he commented, tilting his own head. "Now try to stay still."

The moment he told her to stay still, Kate wanted to move. She hadn't realized that holding a pose would be difficult, even if it was an easy pose. Kaliq was already scratching away with his pencil, though. He'd pause to take peeks at her, then work on his paper, then look at her again. Several minutes passed without a word between them.

"I didn't realize this was going to be such a serious endeavor," Kate tried to lighten the mood. Kaliq's brows were furrowed in concentration and he chewed absentmindedly on his lower lip.

"Don't move."

"Yes, sir," Kate smirked. "I just wanted to get a little more comfortable."

"You're uncomfortable?" Kaliq looked concerned.

"A little," Kate admitted, her lips spreading into a mischievous grin. "My arm is falling asleep."

Kaliq examined the work he'd done. "Okay, how about this. We take a five minute break, then continue?"

Kate stretched and yawned. "Can I see?" she reached for the pad of paper in Kaliq's lap.

"Not yet!" he exclaimed, snatching it just out of her reach. "It's not done yet. You have to let me finish."

"Okay, okay!" Kate was surprised by Kaliq's reaction. If she hadn't known any better, she would have thought he was panicking.

"I just don't want you to see it before it's ready," Kaliq explained. "I don't want you to be disappointed."

Oh my God, Kate thought. *I know that look. I know that expression on his face. It's insecurity.* How was it possible that even someone in Kaliq al Abbas' position dealt with insecurities? He was rich, smart, handsome, charming, powerful, and so many other positive adjectives, many of which Kate didn't feel she could use to describe herself.

"I'm probably going to love it simply based on the fact that it's the only portrait of me that anyone's ever drawn," Kate tried to assuage Kaliq's fears. "I'm sure it's really good though," she added when she realized that her first comment wasn't exactly a vote of confidence.

"I hope you like it," Kaliq looked down at his work. "I've just got to work out the shading."

Kate was now dying to see Kaliq's work. There was no way in hell that she would have not liked it. Even if he had drawn a stick figure, she probably would have been thrilled. "Okay, break over," she announced, shifting back into position so that he'd get back to work.

Kaliq adjusted her until she was in exactly the same position. The warm desert air kissed her skin and the faint sound of men speaking in Arabic drifted through the tent's walls as Kaliq scratched away with his pencil.

Kate felt surprisingly relaxed and comfortable. Just a month prior, she never would have believed that she'd be able to feel so at ease completely naked in front of a man. She would have obsessed over her hips and thighs, which she felt were disproportionately thick compared to the rest of her. She also would have wanted to pose in some position that made her boobs look bigger. Maybe with her arms crossed in front of her so that she could try to squeeze them together to make some cleavage.

In front of Kaliq, though, Kate felt beautiful and sexy. Even when he was poring over every tiny detail of her figure rather than making love to her, she didn't feel judged or inadequate. It was obvious to her that Kaliq liked what he saw, freckles and all.

"I've almost got it here," he mentioned, tilting his head and examining his work. "There's something missing still, but I can't figure out what."

"If you show me, I might be able to help," Kate offered.

"No! You can't see until I'm done. Stop trying to trick me," Kaliq joked.

"Jeez, okay. Just offering," Kate grinned sheepishly.

Kaliq wrinkled his nose and rubbed the pad of his thumb on the paper. Then he did a little more work with his pencil and nodded to himself. "Okay I think this is it."

"Can I look now?"

"Yeah. This is just a quick sketch," Kaliq

warned, reluctant to hand over the pad. "I'd like to put more detail in or even turn it into a big oil piece, if you like it."

Kate waited patiently for Kaliq to show her his work. "That would be cool," she added. "Can I see your sketch?"

Finally Kaliq set his lips in a determined line and handed the pad over. "I can fix any part you don't like," he offered, before Kate could even see what he had drawn.

Kate grabbed the notepad before he could change his mind and stall any longer. "Oh my God," she muttered as soon as she saw his work.

"God, I'm sorry. This was a dumb idea," Kaliq immediately replied, trying to grab the pad back. "Don't be angry."

"Stop!" Kate had to roll away to prevent Kaliq from snatching his drawing back. "I'm not angry! It's beautiful! I'm just surprised because it doesn't look anything like me. It's like the movie star version of me."

It was true. Kaliq's drawing was sexy.

Kate could recognize herself, but everything about the Kate in Kaliq's drawing was just a little better than the real Kate. Her breasts were perkier, her hips were rounder, her nose was more button-y, and her lips were fuller. "Thank you for making me hot." Kate couldn't peel her eyes off Kaliq's version of her.

"I didn't make you hot," he protested. "I just drew what I saw."

"Oh come on," Kate smiled. "This lady is hot," she waved the notepad at Kaliq. "This is the lady who plays me in the televised version of my memoirs. This isn't me in real life. I like it though."

"Kate, I can assure you, that's what you look like in real life. You're absolutely stunning." Kaliq's shocked expression told Kate that he believed what he was saying.

"That's very sweet of you," she assured him, "but I think you must be dreaming. I wish I looked like this drawing."

"Well your wish just came true. I definitely did not idealize you in any way," Kaliq insisted. He rose from the rickety aluminum chair where he was seated and joined Kate on the bed. "I just drew your pretty lips," he said softly, tracing his thumb over her lip, "and your long white neck," he added, his fingers traveling to her throat, "and your sweet tits."

Kate sucked in her breath and arched her back as Kaliq rolled her nipple gently between his thumb and forefinger.

"Think you can handle another round?" he asked quietly, sliding his other hand up her inner thigh.

"Can you?" Kate propped herself up on her elbows and set the notepad aside.

"Oh, I think I can manage," Kaliq replied, sweeping his fingertips across Kate's wet lips.

"Good," Kate grinned and playfully shoved Kaliq back on his heels. "Because I think it's my turn to torture you a little."

"Torture me?" Kaliq laughed. "What did I do to deserve that? My drawing wasn't that bad, was it?"

"On the contrary, the drawing is great. I just think I owe you a little payback for being such a tease earlier. I seem to recall you making me practically beg you for release about an hour ago."

"Oh, that," Kaliq joked. "I wouldn't really say that I *made* you beg. Maybe you're just a greedy, greedy girl," his lips curled into a smile.

"Oh I'm about to show you how greedy I am," Kate purred back, taking his cock in her small hand. He was warm, and smooth, and as hard as a rock. Kate just had to get a taste of him. She brought her lips up to his smooth head and gave it a few ladylike licks. "Mmm," she moaned. She dipped her tongue out and swirled it around the tip of Kaliq's penis. She could feel his thigh tense up underneath her free hand, but he didn't make a sound.

"Katie…" he whispered as she took the head of his cock into her mouth. "You don't have to…"

"I want to," she answered, taking his cock out of her mouth for just a moment before getting back to work. She pressed her tongue against the underside of his head and slowly took him a bit deeper into her mouth. Kate had to stretch her lips to get them wrapped around Kaliq and she knew that her jaw would probably be sore before she was through with what she wanted to do to him, but his reaction was worth the pain.

Kaliq had very gently laid one hand on the back of Kate's head. He didn't apply any pressure, but just the presence of his large palm on her crown made Kate feel like she had to take him deeper in her throat. She sucked his head and slid her hand up and down the rest of his shaft, using the wetness of her mouth as a natural lubricant.

Kate could already taste beads of pre cum forming at the tip of Kaliq's cock, and she lapped these away eagerly as she sped up her pace. She could hear Kaliq breathing heavily and the sound of him trying to control himself was so hot to her. Her own fingers slid toward her sex, where she lightly traced circles around her still-sensitive clit.

"Katie, that's going to make me cum," Kaliq warned, his voice an octave higher than normal.

"Good," Kate replied before setting to work in earnest, sucking him with all of her might and sliding her hand rapidly up and down his shaft, giving her wrist a slight twist.

Kaliq couldn't be quiet any longer. He groaned and pushed Kate's head down, gagging her a little bit before he sprayed a stream of hot, salty cream into her throat. "Oh God Katie," he cried out as his dick twitched in her mouth.

When she was sure he was spent, Kate sat up and wiped her mouth with the back of her hand. "Was that okay for you?" she asked, though she could tell by the way he gazed at the ceiling while trying to catch his breath that she'd blown his mind.

"Yeah," he managed to pant. "Come here."

Kaliq pulled Kate into his arms and they collapsed onto her cot together. He kissed the top of her head and squeezed her small body tightly against his own. He was covered in a thin layer of sweat and the woodsy scent of his body filled the air in her small tent. "Yeah," he repeated, "that was pretty fucking okay."

Kate smiled like the cat that got the cream. She nestled up against Kaliq and let sleep come over her, filling her head with dreams about him and her and all the things they would do together. She dozed off looking forward to what the morning might have in store.

16

"Um, Kate? Dr. Delaney?"

Kate's eyelids fluttered against the bright morning sun. She was hot and sticky, covered in sweat, and squished against the wall of her tent.

"Kate?" a nervous male voice repeated. "I'm really sorry to bother you but we're kind of having an emergency."

Kate blinked her eyes and tried to figure out where she was and what was happening. Then she heard a deep snore and remembered everything. She was in bed with Kaliq. They had spent the night together and it must have been early. Either that or they had overslept.

"Dr. Delaney? I'm really, really sorry but we really need you right now. Please wake up."

"Mike?" Kate asked, rubbing the sleep from her eyes. She began to sit up, but then she realized she was still naked and Kaliq had most of her blanket.

"Kate! Oh my God. I'm really sorry to butt in here, but it's an emergency. We need you out at the lamassu. That General is here and he says that everyone is under arrest. Please, please do something."

"What?!?" This time Kate did bolt upright, stealing the blanket from Kaliq, who was still sleeping peacefully next to her. Mike's eyes flicked to the naked man, then back to Kate. He had evidently made a snap decision to pretend not to notice Kaliq in Kate's bed, and for that Kate would be eternally grateful. "Give me ten seconds to get dressed, and I'll meet you at Fred and Barney."

Mike ran off and Kate jumped over Kaliq's slumbering frame, taking just a moment to pull on pants, a shirt, and her boots. "Kaliq?" she shook him. He rolled over onto his back and snored even more loudly. "Kaliq?" she yelled this time, rocking his body back and forth.

He was still out cold. Kate decided that she didn't have time to keep trying to rouse him. She kissed his sleeping cheek and made a run for it to the dig.

When she got there, she could see a number of men in military uniforms gathered at the lookout point, following instructions shouted by a man who looked like a smaller version of the General al Hamar she had seen on TV. The little general was down at the base of the lamassu, instructing the men in Arabic and ignoring Jarrod Cole, who was beside him yelling about something that Kate couldn't quite make out yet.

"What is going on here?" she asked, joining Jarrod and the small general. "What is this?"

"Who is in charge here?" the general demanded, ignoring Jarrod. "Where is the man in charge?"

"I'm the lead archaeologist on this dig," Kate answered, ignoring the request for a man.

"Who is your boss?" the general asked.

"I'm in charge here," Kate clarified. "I answer to the Sheikha al Abbas, but she isn't present."

The general looked Kate up and down, rolled his eyes, and gave an exasperated sigh. "So you are in charge? Fine. You are under arrest."

"Under whose authority?" Kate demanded.

This got the man's attention. He glared at her for a moment as if sizing her up. "Mine. You and your people were given fair warning. Despite what the thieving al Abbas clan may have told you, these idols are on Sanaari land. They're a black mark on Sanaari culture and they're coming down, today."

"So you're General al Hamar?" Kate asked, surprised. He looked so much less threatening in real life than he did on film.

"Yes, and I'm here representing the people of Sanaar. Please order your crew to back away a minimum of twenty meters so that no one gets hurt."

"Why would anyone get hurt?" Kate asked, the suspicion rising in her voice. What were those soldiers doing up at the lookout? They appeared to be coating Fred's neck in some kind of white gum.

"Madame, you had warning. These idols have been oppressing the people of Sanaar for long enough, and it's past time they came down. Please tell your people to back up."

"What's going on here?" a familiar voice boomed from behind them. Kate turned to see Kaliq running towards her, fully dressed.

The General yelled something up to his soldiers and they began to make their way back down through the tunnel.

Kate could tell by Kaliq's expression that he was alarmed by whatever the General had said. He and the General had a brief and angry exchange in Arabic that ended in Kaliq calling the General a psycho.

"You're the one spending a fortune to preserve these monstrosities," the General snapped at Kaliq. "But that's irrelevant now, you can save your money. They're coming down. Now I highly recommend that you step back unless you want to go down with them."

Kaliq sighed and wrapped his arm around Kate's waist, pulling her back.

"Wait, what? What's going on right now?" Kate demanded, shocked that Kaliq was apparently willing to stand by and let this megalomaniacal little man bulldoze antiquities.

"We've fucked up. I'm sorry Katie, but we're too late. Hamar's already got your statue rigged. That's C4 stuck to it; he's going to blow it up."

"What?" Katie shrieked. "No," she cried.

"There's nothing we can do, sweetheart. I

need to keep you safe."

Maybe there was nothing that Kaliq thought that he could do, but Kate wasn't going to just stand there while General Asshole blew up a pair of irreplaceable treasures. Kate slipped from Kaliq's grip and made a run for the entrance to the tunnels.

"Kate! Stop!" she heard Kaliq cry out behind her.

She hated to put Kaliq in a difficult spot, but she had no choice. Kate made a mad dash for the tunnels and hoped that the General wouldn't be crazy enough to detonate his explosives and blow her up.

Kate ran into the tunnels and up, up, up to the lookout. If she could just get to the area where she had seen the soldiers working, she could remove the explosives they'd affixed to Fred and Kaliq could talk some sense into the General. She could hear the heavy thud of a single pair of boots behind her, but light as she was, there was no way that a single pursuer could keep up with her or even catch her.

Kate was almost to the lookout when it happened. She didn't even hear anything. She was knocked flat on her back and the world was silent. Then the ground was shaking beneath her and everything got darker. She couldn't even tell if there was something weird happening to the light in the tunnel or whether she was blacking out.

She didn't know how much time passed, it could have been seconds or it could have been minutes, but gradually her entire back started to ache. It was a dull pain at first, one that spread from her tailbone to her shoulders, but with every beat of her heart, the pain got more intense.

Kate wiggled one foot, then the other, just to make sure that she still could. Slowly, she sat up and looked around. Her back was sore, but she didn't seem to be seriously injured. Plus, she could just start to hear her own blood pumping in her ears, so she wasn't deaf either.

"Kate?" she heard a familiar voice. "Kate are you okay?"

"Oh my God, Kaliq? Is that you?" Kate

looked around but she couldn't see anyone else. Part of the tunnel seemed to have collapsed and the way back down was filled with rocks and debris.

"Kate?" Kaliq called back from behind a boulder. "Are you hurt? Stay put, I'll come rescue you."

"I'm not hurt," Kate finally stood up and began to make her way to the voice. "Are you okay?"

"I'm a little sore," Kaliq admitted as soon as Kate found him, "but I'm not injured."

"Kaliq," Kate rushed to respond, "I'm so sorry. I didn't mean for you to get stuck in here with me. I didn't think he'd really do it."

"I'm the one who owes you an apology," Kaliq hugged Kate, glad she seemed alright. "I promised I would protect you and your lamassu and look where we are now. To be honest, I didn't really think he would detonate either. He really is insane."

"I can't believe he blew up the lamassu while you were in the tunnel. What if he had killed you? Your family is going to be pissed." Kate hoped that they didn't blame her. She guessed she was getting ahead of herself though, since they hadn't even actually escaped the tunnel alive yet. "You think he's still out there?"

"I don't know," Kaliq considered the question. "My first instinct is that he probably didn't want to hang around and wait for my family or my security forces to arrive. Any one of my brothers would have probably killed him on the spot if they believed he'd murdered me. My private security should be here any minute now too, since they take over from the night shift at six AM. I don't know for sure what this guy is doing, though, since he's obviously crazy. Maybe he does want to start some kind of war with Samarra."

"You think he's looking for us right now?"

Kaliq looked around the cave. The exit to the lookout was buried in rubble. Some of the electric lights were still working, but there was no telling how long they'd be on. "Probably not. I think he'd have probably found us by now if he'd followed us in. He's probably afraid of the tunnels collapsing on him."

Kate and Kaliq both took a good look around. "I guess these tunnels weren't as secure as the engineering team thought," Kate observed.

"Well, in the engineers' defense, they probably weren't expecting these tunnels to be blown up. Anyhow, we'd better get out of here. I'm not so sure that these walls will continue to hold."

Kate knew Kaliq was right. She could still hear the sound of stray rocks falling from the walls. Every once in a while, they'd hear a small crash, as though a wall might have given in. They didn't know what they'd have to face once they got out of the tunnel, but it was almost certainly not as dangerous as what they were facing in the tunnel.

The pair made their way down the winding path that led back to the front exit. There were several spots where they had to either climb over large rocks or squeeze through tight spaces.

"Can you make it?" Kate asked Kaliq at one such passage. A large boulder had come loose from one wall and was leaned up against the opposite wall. Kate could easily slip under the space left between the boulder and the wall, but Kaliq was much bigger.

"I think we're gonna have to dig under a little."

Kaliq pulled back a few of the larger stones that had rolled beneath the boulder and Kate kicked away the smaller debris. Even after they'd made the hole bigger, though, it was still too small.

"I'm afraid that if we remove too much ground, this boulder's gonna fall," Kaliq admitted.

"Okay," Kate smoothed back her hair. "Here's what we're gonna do. I'll squeeze through, go get help, and bring back the engineers. They'll know how to dig you out safely."

"Are you sure you'll be okay on your own?" Kaliq asked.

"Yeah, I've been through these tunnels a million times and I know them like the back of my hand. Plus I can move faster without you," she smiled, teasing Kaliq a bit to lighten the mood.

"Okay. If Hamar is still out there and he gives you a hard time, just try to stall until my brothers arrive. I'm pretty sure that they've been contacted and they're on their way."

Kate gave Kaliq a long, deep kiss. "I'll be right back for you," she assured him, before jogging off into the dark tunnel alone.

17

It wasn't long before Kate realized that
the tunnels were in far worse condition than she
had realized. The loose boulder blocking Kaliq's
way was only the first in a series of collapsed
zones that Kate had to either climb over or
through. In several spots, she had to slow down

and take her time carefully removing debris that blocked her way.

She was almost glad that Kaliq couldn't see what she was doing, since it was treacherous work. Every time she removed a larger stone, the smaller rocks resettled and sometimes more of the tunnel's wall would collapse. Kate had to carefully examine each pile of debris in her path before she touched anything in order to avoid moving a rock that would cause a huge piece of the wall to fall.

A passage that ordinarily would have taken Kate ten minutes to traverse took thirty. She hoped that Kaliq wasn't panicking back there alone in the tunnels. The electric lights were still holding out, so at least he wasn't stuck in the dark.

Kate reached a point in the tunnel where the way way blocked with a tower of large boulders that all seemed to be loose. She tested them gently with her hand. She could tell by the way they barely moved under her touch that they were held in place by tension, and when she moved one, more would fall from the wall.

She took a step back and wiped the sweat from her forehead on her shirtsleeve, leaving a smear of grime on her white shirt. She was hot, tired, and filthy. She'd give her left arm for a nice, long, hot shower and she desperately needed a sip of water. Kate knew that they'd need to get out of that tunnel soon, before they started to really feel the effects of dehydration, and she hoped that the air quality was okay.

Motivated by her thirst, she looked the boulders over, stepped back as far as she could, and gave one of the stones in the middle a kick. The entire tower came toppling down so that she had to jump back to avoid them, and a large portion of the wall came down too.

Once everything had settled, she tested the debris on the ground and discovered that her plan had worked. The new pile of rocks was just a pile rather than a precariously balanced stack. She'd be able to climb over without worrying about them collapsing on her.

Kate wondered whether the state of the

tunnel indicated that al Hamar had set explosives inside too, rather than just on the lamassu. The idea brought her thoughts back to Fred and Barney and she wondered how bad the damage was. There hadn't been a series of explosions, thank God, so she was hoping that it couldn't have been that bad. She wasn't exactly an explosives expert though, so she was eager to see their condition.

The further she got in the tunnel, the worse the passage became. Kate had to pause to take breaks frequently and she was getting pretty scratched up and bruised from having to clamber over and through the rubble. She didn't want to overexert herself because she wasn't sure what waited ahead, but the more damage she saw, the more concerned she became.

Finally, she recognized from a turn in the tunnel that she was almost through. She was a bit surprised by how quiet everything was. She had expected to hear more yelling, or maybe the engines of the trucks that would inevitably be cleaning up the mess.

Kate hoped that al Hamar hadn't really arrested everyone. She had no idea what she'd have to do in order to bail her entire staff out of jail in Sanaar. She was pretty certain that al Hamar wouldn't be able to hold everyone indefinitely, but it would probably take some effort from the local US embassy to get things rolling.

As Kate progressed through the tunnel, fewer and fewer live lamps lit her way. Most of the remaining lamps near the tunnel's entrance were blown out, and some stretches were so dark that she had to feel her way along to make sure she didn't trip. Some of the broken lamps hung from the walls, dangling by electric cords that must have still been live, since the lamps deeper in the tunnel were still on.

Kate knew, in her heart, what to expect before she saw. The increased damage, the busted lamps, and the silence all pointed to one possibility. She just hadn't wanted to accept that possibility, which is why she was still shocked and disappointed when reality hit her in the face.

"No," she whimpered, feeling the solid mass in front of her. "Fuck, fuck fuck, no," but there was no denying what she was feeling. The entrance to the tunnels was completely caved in. It wasn't even blocked with a few large stones that could potentially be moved. It was filled with a mix of large boulders, small rocks, and dirt that formed a solid wall.

Kate release a string of curses that would have made a sailor blush when her hand passed over what she was pretty sure was a giant, solid sandstone nose. So Hamar had blown Fred's nose off, and possibly his entire head. Could it be repaired? She had absolutely no idea. At the very least, the loose pieces could be displayed safely in a museum.

If Kate hadn't been on the brink of panicking over her current predicament, she would have been beside herself over the damage done to the lamassu. As things stood, however, she needed to find a way out of the tunnels before the lack of water and possibly fresh air did serious damage to her and Kaliq.

Hopefully, her friends and colleagues were on the other side of that wall of rock, rather than being driven to a Sanaari prison. Hopefully, they hadn't immediately assumed that she and Kaliq were dead. Hopefully, someone was on the way with the equipment needed to safely open a passage to the tunnels.

None of those hopes were guarantees, though, and she and Kaliq couldn't afford to wait around and hope to be rescued. She wasn't even sure that the tunnel was still safe. For all she knew, it could be on the brink of collapse.

Kate made her way back to Kaliq with a heavy heart. She felt terribly guilty about getting him stuck in this mess, and she dreaded having to tell him about how fucked they really were.

"Kaliq?" she called out softly when she finally got close to the spot where she'd left him. "You still there?"

"Katie?" she heard him respond. Then she heard some shuffling, like maybe he'd been sitting down and he stood up. "What's happening out there."

Kate approached him and couldn't hide the disappointment on her face. "The tunnel collapsed," she admitted, wrapping her arms around his waist.

"Shit! Are you okay?"

"Oh no," Kate hurried to clarify, "it didn't collapse on me. It was already a wreck. The entrance is blocked. And Fred's head got blown off."

"The lamassu?" Kaliq sounded apprehensive.

"Yeah," Kate replied.

"At least no people were hurt, as far as we know," Kaliq tried to comfort her.

"Not yet at least." Kate didn't want to be a total Debbie Downer, but she was struggling to remain positive in the situation.

"Okay, we need to find another way out of here," Kaliq's voice changed. He didn't sound like he was making a suggestion, he sounded like he was giving an order. Kate was glad that he was willing to lead, because she was honestly not feeling very confident in herself. "Is there another exit that you know of?" Kaliq asked her.

"No, just the two. We haven't been through the tunnels though. The engineers were really strict about not allowing anybody into areas of the tunnels that they hadn't cleared as safe."

"How dangerous are the uncleared tunnels?"

"I don't know. I've only checked them out a little bit. The one I saw seemed okay, but who knows about stuff like air quality."

Kaliq considered what Kate was saying. "Well, it's not like we know for sure that we're safe here now either. I'm sure my family is doing everything possible to get us out of here, but there's no telling how long that could take or whether the tunnel will completely collapse when that debris is hauled away. I think we need to try to find another way out."

Kate nodded. "You're right. Those tunnels aren't lit though."

"Fuck. Do you have a phone?"

"Yeah, but our phones don't get reception

in here."

"Does your phone have a flashlight?"

"Oh, duh, yes," Kate answered, fishing around in her pocket.

"Don't turn it on yet," Kaliq warned when she found it. "We should wait until we absolutely need them so we don't run the batteries down."

"Okay," Kate looked up into Kaliq's green eyes, which reflected the light that shone from the lamps that dimly lit the tunnel they were in.

"You ready?" Kaliq asked, stroking her cheek with his thumb.

Kate nodded and set off with Kaliq right behind her. They headed back up the path toward the lookout, but then instead of continuing the way they had come from, they made a turn that took them to the long, straight tunnel that Kate had already poked around.

The "Do Not Cross" tape that had tempted Kate only a few days prior now looked ominous. She pulled it down and stepped over it with Kaliq, into the black tunnel that burrowed deeper into the mountain.

"You've been in here?" Kaliq asked her.

Kate nodded. "Not all the way. This tunnel goes on and on and I never found out what was at the other end."

"Okay. It looks like this tunnel just goes deep into the mountain. Do other tunnels intersect?"

"Not that I encountered. When I went in, it was a straight shot about the length of a football field. I was looking for possible housing or storage, but the tunnel goes so deep into the mountain that it's unlikely that anyone was able to live back there. There's no telling what we'll find."

"We need a plan. We'll head in, follow the path, and turn right if we encounter any options. If we don't find an additional exit and we start getting short of breath, we'll turn back and wait for rescue here."

"All right," Kate agreed. Kaliq's plan was good. Any passage to the right was likely to lead out of the mountain.

They agreed to use the light from one

phone at a time to stretch the batteries as long as possible and they slowly made their way down the tunnel. The further they got from the explosion site, the clearer the path was. It was actually a pretty easy stroll compared to the journey Kate had made to the tunnel's entry.

"How long did you say this passage was?" Kaliq asked, shining the weak light from his phone's flashlight into the black darkness ahead.

"At least the size of a football field. The last time I came in here I walked and walked and never reached even a turn."

"How are you feeling?"

"Fine, actually."

"Me too. I'm pretty sure that there must be another way out up here somewhere because the air quality is too good for this tunnel to be completely closed off. We just need to keep going and eventually we'll find it."

Kate appreciated Kaliq's positive outlook, and his reasoning made sense to her. They'd just keep hiking, and eventually this path would spit them out on the side of the mountain.

Kate was feeling so good about their prospects that she picked up her pace. She strode up the trail they were following, eager to find that secret exit they'd imagined. The faster she walked, the faster they'd be out, she reasoned.

She was practically at a jog when the toe of her boot caught on something and she ate dirt. Kaliq tried to catch her but he wasn't quick enough. Kate ended up on the ground with a sharp pain shooting through her ankle.

18

"I'm okay," Kate tried to assure Kaliq, scrambling to her feet as fast as possible. Unfortunately, it was immediately clear to them both that she wasn't okay. Her left ankle wouldn't support her weight. "Maybe I just need to rest for a second."

Kate leaned against the wall of the tunnel and rubbed her ankle. It was tender to the touch and hot. She had probably sprained it.

"Kate?" Kaliq asked gently. "Did you twist it?"

"Ugh, maybe? I don't know. I think it'll be okay." Kate didn't want to screw things up any worse than she already had. She tried to stand up again and caught herself before she fell over.

"It's okay. It'll be okay," Kaliq assured her. "Look," he swept her up into his arms, "I can just carry you."

"Kaliq," Kate laughed for the first time in several hours, "you can't carry me all the way through this dark tunnel. I'm too heavy. You'll break your back."

"I promise that you're not too heavy. I'm a big guy! It's really no trouble."

"Seriously, though, you can just leave me here, go get help, then come back and get me." Actually the thought of being left alone in a pitch black tunnel in the middle of the mountain terrified Kate, but she didn't see any other option. If both she and Kaliq were injured, they would be in seriously deep shit. She'd just have to suck it up, quit being a baby, and tough it out until Kaliq could find some help.

"Kate, I'm not going to leave you here. That's crazy. What if I get lost in here? We need to stick together." Kaliq looked around the dark tunnel. "Plus, I think I can hear bats flapping around. I'm not going to leave you here in the dark with a bunch of disgusting winged rats."

"Well, since you put it that way," Kate agreed. Plus, it seemed like her weight really wasn't much of a burden to Kaliq. He was barely exerting himself. "You want me to hold the flashlight?"

Kaliq handed her his phone and she lit the way from her spot in his arms. He held her tightly against his chest and they barely slowed down. They had already proceeded long past the point Kate had visited before. Or at least Kate believed they were much further, since they seemed to have been walking for a long time.

They trudged through the dark tunnel for what seemed like hours, Kaliq shifting Kate's weight from one arm to the other. Kate's ankle throbbed with a dull ache, but as long as she tried to keep her foot from bumping against anything, she was okay.

"Does the air seem different to you?" Kaliq asked, stopping to sniff.

Kate took a deep breath. "You mean, like, less mildewy?" She inhaled through her nose again. "Yes. I think it does."

"Yes. Finally. That means there's fresh air coming in somewhere nearby. We're going to get out of here."

It seemed to make sense. Kate would have felt a little better if she could see light coming in from somewhere, but fresh air was a start. Before they could find what they were looking for, the flashlight on Kaliq's phone flickered out. Kate rifled through her pocket and retrieved her own phone.

The flashlight on her phone was quite a bit brighter than Kaliq's. It was so bright, in fact, that it illuminated another passage to the right of the one they were following.

"Shit," Kaliq commented. "I hope we

haven't been walking past exits for the past half hour." He turned on his heel and promptly proceeded through the new entry.

Just inside the door, Kate's foot knocked something that seemed to have been set on a shelf at about waist height. They heard a clatter and Kate instinctively shined the flashlight on the ground to check out what they'd bumped into.

"Oh my God," Kaliq jumped back, almost dropping Kate.

It was a skull. And it had fallen off a shelf lined with dozens more.

"Oh my God," Kate repeated. But whereas Kaliq's 'oh my God' was an expression of shock and possibly disgust, Kate's 'oh my God' was quite the opposite. She was absolutely thrilled. "This is what I've been looking for," she muttered, almost as much to herself as to Kaliq, "it's a tomb!"

"You *wanted* to find a bunch of creepy skeletons?" Kaliq's eyebrows went up.

"Well not necessarily skeletons," Kate explained. "But something. Anything that might teach us the original use of these tunnels. I've been looking for evidence of living quarters or storage, but the more I think about it, the more a tomb makes sense."

Kate shone her flashlight around the small room they were standing in, illuminating row after row of bones. "This is great," she muttered under her breath. "This turned out to be the best thing that's ever happened to me."

"See?" Kaliq laughed. "I'm making all of your dreams come true. Now if we could just find where that fresh air is coming from, we could get out of here and you could dazzle all of the less intrepid archaeologists with your find."

"Well," Kate looked around, "I'm guessing that there may be some sort of ventilation shaft in this room. We might be able to find it and crawl through."

"Or we could use that door," Kaliq gestured with his chin to an opening in the wall on the other side of the room.

"Or we could use the door," Kate nodded in agreement, breathing a sigh of relief that she wouldn't actually have to crawl through any tight spaces with her busted ankle. "Do you need a break?" she asked Kaliq, remembering that he was the one who'd been carrying her since her mishap.

"Nah," he replied, gazing around the small, crowded room. "Who do you think these people were?"

"Possibly priests. They must have held some important position if they were buried in this tomb, but it doesn't look quite luxurious enough for them to be royalty. We'll have to come back with lights and equipment."

"Come back?" Kaliq laughed. "No thanks. I'll leave the tomb raiding to you. You can spend the day geeking out over these skulls and then give me the low down over dinner," he teased.

Kate had to admit, getting excited over a room full of centuries-old skulls was pretty dorky. She didn't feel like Kaliq was judging her for it, though. His teasing was good natured. He was probably happy that they were going to get out of that tunnel without any more disasters. God knew Kate was thrilled.

The door on the other side of the room led into another passageway, but it was obvious that this one led to an exit because there was a light breeze. The tunnel smelled like desert air rather than mildew.

It wasn't long before they could see the light at the end of the tunnel. Kaliq's pace picked up and soon they could both see the midday sun pouring through a small exit in the side of the mountain.

"We're free!" Kate exclaimed.

Kaliq looked around the desert where they had emerged. The camp was nowhere in site. "I wonder how long we've been walking."

"It seemed like a long time. I don't recognize where we are."

"Are either of the phones getting reception?"

Kate glanced at the phone still in her hand. "Not this one. And the other one has a dead battery."

"Okay, I don't think we should try to walk back in this sun. Let's take a break here, then when the sun passes over the mountain and we're in the shade, we'll make our way back to camp."

Kate agreed. She remembered what Kaliq was like when she first met him, when he was suffering from dehydration and heat exhaustion. The desert could be a dangerous place, and she was already incapacitated. They didn't have any water, and despite what he was saying, Kaliq probably needed a break from carrying her.

"Should we head back into the tomb? Maybe we could start cataloguing those bodies?"

Kaliq gave Kate a look like she had completely lost her mind.

"I was just kidding," she laughed. "Put me down. We're probably gonna be here for a couple hours."

Kaliq set Kate on her butt near the entrance of the tunnel, just where the shade began, then took a seat next to her. They leaned up against the stone wall and Kate stretched her injured leg out.

"How's it feeling?" Kaliq asked.

"A little sore. I'll probably just need to stay off it for a while."

"I'm sorry I got you into this."

"*You're* sorry," Kate turned to Kaliq. "How could you be sorry? This is all my fault."

"I promised you that I'd protect you and your work and you've got a bum leg and your statue is missing his head."

"None of that is your fault."

"I just wanted you to see that I'm not a useless rich guy who relies on his family to get whatever he wants."

"What? I never thought that. Why would I think that?"

"People tend to make assumptions when you've got a family like mine. My youngest brother's still in school, but both of my other brothers are pillars of the community. Amir's some kind of business tycoon and Nasir is a human rights attorney. I'm kind of the black sheep here."

"Is that why you didn't tell me who you were when we first met?"

"I just wanted to be treated like an ordinary guy."

"You're not an ordinary guy. You're a babe. I can see your point though."

Kaliq smiled and gave Kate a warm kiss. She'd never considered what it would be like to belong to a family like his. She'd always just assumed that it must be great to always get whatever you wanted, whether that was an opportunity or some material thing. It had never occurred to her that Kaliq felt an immense pressure to live up to everyone's expectations.

Kate nestled up to Kaliq and gazed out upon the sandy expanses. The searing midday sun caused visible waves of heat to rise from the dry ground, and the sky was so intensely blue that it looked unreal.

"It really is beautiful out here," Kate observed, her eyelids getting heavy.

"You think so?" Kaliq seemed surprised. "I've always been partial to forests myself."

19

"Katie, wake up baby."

Kate squinted and blinked her eyes against the light seeping in. Her back ached and her entire leg throbbed with a dull pain. She seemed to be sitting in some sort of cave. She looked around and spotted Kaliq squatted next to her. There were also two other men there who she didn't recognize.

Then it all came back. The explosion, the adventure through the tunnels, the twisted ankle, the tomb. All of it.

"Here," Kaliq lifted a flask to her lips. "Drink this."

Kate gulped down the water he offered her and looked over the two strange men. They both looked vaguely familiar, but the jeans and undershirts they both wore suggested to Kate that they weren't Hamar's soldiers or there in any kind of official capacity.

"Are we under arrest?" Kate asked, just to make sure.

"Yes," the guy with shorter hair replied. "Get in the truck."

"Don't be an asshole," Kaliq retorted.

Ah. Kate recognized that type of exchange. These men were siblings.

"Are you hurt?" the other man asked Kate, taking a look at her ankle.

"I think it's just a twisted ankle, or maybe a sprain."

"We'll have my wife look at it. She used

to be a doctor."

"Michelle?" Kate remembered meeting the very nice, very pregnant woman at the al Abbas' party.

"Yes. You can recuperate at my house and we'll take care of you. I'm Amir, by the way." Kaliq's brother offered Kate his hand to shake. "And this is my brother Nasir."

Nasir didn't offer her a handshake or even look at her. "Are you two ready?" he asked Kaliq. "Because I wasn't really planning to spend my entire day in this cave."

Kaliq ignored his brother and addressed Kate in a low voice. "Let's get out of here." He picked her up and carried her to a waiting Land Rover, depositing her in the back before climbing in after her.

The inside of the car was nothing like the outside. Whereas the outside looked like a rugged all-terrain vehicle, the inside looked like some sort of luxurious lounge. Four creamy white leather seats faced one another and between each pair of seats, Kate spotted a console that included a number of buttons to control the climate, music, and lighting, plus a small refrigerator.

This car was definitely more along the lines of what Kate pictured when she thought "billionaire." She slid into the buttery soft leather seat and sipped on a cool bottle of water Kaliq handed her from the fridge. "Is this yours?" she finally asked.

"This car? No. Noooooo. This is Amir's," Kaliq laughed. "He's kind of a flashy guy. Nasir too. Not really my style."

It didn't look like Kaliq's style, but it was nice for a change. "How did they find us?" Kate wondered aloud.

"Amir tracked my phone. My security detail showed up shortly after Hamar detonated those explosions and they contacted my brothers right away. Your engineers were trying to clear the tunnel with their equipment, but Amir figured out that we were out here."

"So everyone didn't get arrested?" Kate breathed a sigh of relief.

"Just our friend Dr. Cole," Kaliq smirked.

"He finally got to take credit for leading the dig."

Kate knew that she shouldn't laugh, but she couldn't help herself. "We're bailing him out, right?"

"Oh, I don't know," Kaliq drawled. "He can probably handle this himself, right? Maybe he doesn't want our help."

"Believe me," Kate assured Kaliq, "no one alive has more interest in dropping Jarrod down a hole and leaving him there forever. But I can't. The entire project would suffer. Oh! By the way, what's happening at the dig now?"

"Hamar fled almost immediately after trying to blow us up, from what I understand. I'm not surprised. He doesn't really have the resources to invade Samarra." Kaliq draped an arm around Kate. "I'm sorry Katie, but it looks like work on the lamassu is on pause indefinitely until this situation gets sorted."

Kate sighed. "I suspected as much."

"Don't worry, Katie," Kaliq stroked her cheek. "You're a great archaeologist. You're so committed to your work, and you just found that tomb. This political bullshit is just a minor setback."

Kate sat back in her seat and thought about her situation. Kaliq was probably right about the site. After finding that tomb, Kate was sure that she'd eventually get to return to her site to continue with her work. She just didn't know what was going to happen to her in the immediate future.

"You're worried?" Kaliq recognized the expression on Kate's face.

"A little," she admitted. "I just don't know what's going to happen to us now." Kate had only known Kaliq for a few weeks, but the thought of leaving him already broke her heart. They'd been through so much together and she really wanted to give this relationship a shot. That seemed impossible if she was about to be shipped back to the States. "My visa here is only good as long as I'm working. Plus, with the camp shut down, I don't have anywhere to live. Who knows how long it will be before we see each other again."

"Oh, Katie," Kaliq squeezed her knee. "Come live with me. My place is kind of a mess but we could fix it up together. I've got plenty of space. You could do whatever paperwork you have to work on for this dig and I could paint."

Kate wasn't too sure. "Kaliq, you don't have to do this."

"I want to do this. Say you'll give it a shot, Kate. Please?"

She couldn't say no to a request like that. Kate had never lived with a boyfriend before, so this was going to be a new adventure for her. "Okay," she agreed. "But what about a year from now when this stage of the dig is wrapped up?"

"Let's just get married," Kaliq's face lit up. "We can stay here as long as your job lasts, then we'll go to the States or wherever life leads us. Maybe to a big city, or maybe to a forest somewhere. You can be a world famous archaeologist and I'll paint portraits and we'll have a million kids."

"Seriously?" Kate honestly couldn't tell whether Kaliq meant what he was suggesting.

"Why not? I'm not too crazy about living in the desert, Katie, but I love you and I think you love me too. Let's do it. Let's get married. This is officially a proposal. Will you marry me?"

"Yes." Kate knew that she probably should have taken some time to consider that answer, but she wanted this more than she'd ever wanted anything in her entire life. "Yes I will marry you. I'd like to have a wedding with my family though."

"We can do that. We can have whatever kind of wedding you want. Just tell me and I'll make it happen. I promise. And I promise you that this time I won't screw up."

Kate unbuckled her seat belt and slid herself over the center console into Kaliq's lap. She grabbed his face in her hands and planted a deep kiss on his lips, not waiting for him to make the first move. She plunged her tongue into his mouth and wrapped her arms around her future husband.

20

"Am I technically a Sheikha now?" Kate laughed and collapsed onto the hotel room's big, king sized bed.

"Technically yes, your highness," her new husband joined her.

"Does that mean I can issue royal decrees?"

"Anything you say in this hotel room

goes."

"In that case, I order you to remove your pants. And the rest of your clothing." Kate propped herself up on her elbows and grinned at Kaliq.

"Your wish is my command," he stood and worked at the buttons on his shirt, slowly revealing his broad chest.

"Is that so? Then I order you to remove my clothing too."

After Kaliq had undressed himself, he worked at the tight lacing up the back of Kate's dress. He untied the ribbons and loosened her cream colored bodice. Kate took a deep breath and relaxed. Her wedding dress was stunning but she wasn't exactly accustomed to wearing fancy dresses and high heels. Plus her entire body ached from dancing for the past four hours.

"This is sexy," Kaliq observed Kate's satin corset. He placed a trail of light kisses over her neck and bare shoulder. "Did you have fun?" he asked.

"I had a blast," Kate nodded. "Did you?"

"Mm hmm," Kaliq tugged Kate's dress off and let it fall to the floor. "Your family is hilarious."

After much deliberation, Kate had ended up planning a wedding nearly identical to her sisters' backyard shindigs. She could have had anything: a cathedral, a designer gown, an exotic destination party, the al Abbas family would have covered it. But when it came down to what she actually wanted, she couldn't help but to dream of having the same type of huge family party that her sisters had thrown.

"I'm glad they got along so well with your family. I was worried that this would be a low-class affair for your family, but they were all so gracious. Even Nasir. He must have eaten an entire pan of my sister's hotdish."

"I think he genuinely liked it," Kaliq replied. "It was good."

"I guess for you guys this could have been an exotic cultural experience," Kate joked, though it was kind of true. The al Abbas family had billions of dollars. They threw parties that cost hundreds of thousands of dollars, in which the guests were heads of state and occasionally celebrities.

Kate and Kaliq's wedding had been a backyard potluck at her parents' midwestern ranch home. They had put up the decorations themselves the day before and Kaliq's brothers' suits had probably cost more than the rest of the wedding expenses combined.

"I'm going native," Kaliq muttered, kissing the tops of Kate's breasts. He unfastened the hook and eye closures on her corset and freed her breasts, turning his attention to their rosy tips. Kaliq took one Kate's nipples between his lips and sucked gently, sending a chill through her spine.

She ran her fingers through his hair, freeing it from the ponytail holder she had lent him just that morning. Over the past several months while she had wrapped up her work on the dig in Samarra, they had grown closer and closer while sharing Kaliq's flat. They'd fallen into a routine almost immediately, one that involved totally ordinary activities like reading the paper together in bed on the weekends and marathoning their favorite shows weeknights. It had been the happiest time of Kate's life so far.

Things seemed like they were only going to get better. Kate had a job offer at a small liberal arts college in rural Vermont. She'd have a light teaching load and plenty of support for her research. She and Kaliq were looking into buying a refurbished farmhouse that had a barn that they would convert into a studio for him.

Best of all, the farmhouse had six bedrooms. There was plenty of space for the huge family they both wanted. Neither of them could wait to get started building that new family, and as of that night they were trying for a baby.

"Kaliq..." Kate moaned his name as he slipped her out of her giant crinoline.

"Yes Mrs. al Abbas?" Kaliq paused his kisses to smile at her.

"Don't stop," she laughed, and he went right back to work, kissing her hip bones and slipping her panties down.

He kneeled between her knees and pushed her legs apart, exposing her wet pink lips to the room's cool air. Kate's stomach clenched and she shut her eyes, waiting for his lips to brush against her once again.

"Come up here," Kate reached for her new husband. He climbed onto the bed between her legs and gave her a deep, hungry kiss, searching for her tongue with his own and pressing her lips against her teeth. "I want you."

"You've got me," he whispered into her ear as he lined the head of his cock up with her sex. "You've got me."

♥

Dear Reader,

Thank you so much for your continued support! It's avid readers like you who make indie romance series like the *Green-Eyed Sheikhs* possible. Please take a moment to let me know what you thought about Kate and Sheikh Kaliq by leaving me a review on Amazon. We can also be friends on Goodreads or Library Thing!
Please join my mailing list so that I can let you know as soon as the next volume in *The Green-Eyed Sheikhs* series is available. Subscribers get inside info about special promotions, plus they get the chance to enter my monthly giveaways.

Yasmin Porter is a huge fan of chiles rellenos. She also likes big dogs, fancy soaps, and postcards. She would love to be your friend on Goodreads or Library Thing.

Sign up for Yasmin's mailing list so she can let you know when the second book in the *Green-Eyed Sheikhs* series is hot off the presses! Just follow this address: http://eepurl.com/be56-1

Made in the USA
San Bernardino, CA
08 July 2015